I0551730

NETER

Rastari Saga, Volume 1

Ras Heru King

Published by Katalize.net, 2023.

Table of Contents

Exordium..1

Twilight 11

Nativity..23

Exodus..33

PART 2 | The 7 Legends of Krstjah................................47

The Red Sea 49

The Fire Star Crater..55

Sermon on the Mt. 63

Heralds of Rasayana..73

Psalm of Sattvastar 91

The Rising Sun 111

The Risen Sun... 133

PART THREE | The Sanctification of the Kings........................ 141

Fire Island and The Holy Roller 143

Holy Smokes! The Biastar Kachina 155

The Passion of the Holy Ghost 175

Glossary 183

Exordium

Many today continue to believe that the myths, legends, and revered symbols of the indigenous people around the world, and the mystics of all ages, are simply cultural fantasies and superstitions, just as Harry Potter and Marvel heroes are today. However, myths are actually allegorical teachings which convey the moral imperatives of a culture. This is their clear distinction from the mere entertainment of the for-profit culture industries of today; the myths of yesteryear were tools for sustaining and progressing culture, and not simply tools for leisure and mental escape.

The Makushi Indians of the Amazon jungle believe they are the descendants of Makunaima, who is the son of the sun and represents the Pleiades star constellation. The Makushi believe in the concept of '*stkaton*,' their version of universal spirit or energy or ki, and for them this energy comes from the sun. Their myths and stories and ceremonies are all related to the sun and stars, and yet they all obviously teach valuable lessons on how a mature and good Makushi behaves and believes.

The most peculiar belief of the Makushi Indians is that they discovered an entrance to the real underworld. Accounts of their claimed voyage in 1907 are available to anyone after a brief internet search of the topic. While the Makushi story has original components, their story is mysteriously similar to the other stories of the inner earth found throughout the world. The Makushi story involves immense plateaus in underground caves, underground forests lit by sun-like orbs, and amiable reptilian humanoids that guard the gates to the underworld.

I had no knowledge of the Makushi Indians or their culture or any of the myths of the indigenous people of the Amazon region when I found myself amongst them during the Fall of 2018. I had traveled to South America to spend time gathering nature footage in the Amazon jungle. I had also planned on documenting indigenous culture and ceremonies, as my idol Maya Deren had done with Haitian Vodou. I landed in the capital city of Guyana, a country which not only borders Brazil and the Amazon, and is itself comprised of 75% undomesticated jungle, but is also the site of one of history's most infamous cult scandals.

After a week in the capital city, Georgetown, Guyana, I met a beautiful Guyanese woman who I started falling for. Upon discussing my plans to visit the jungle with her, she repeatedly warned me against going into what the locals call 'the interior,' and she frequently detailed the dangers of what they called 'the bush.' However, I was confident in my continuing good fortune and made plans to venture into the wild. After I finalized my travel arrangements and tour guides, I was finally ready to board a van in Georgetown which would take me to a small plane. Just before I entered that van, I kissed my Guyanese girlfriend goodbye, and reassured her that I would be back in no time.

What was supposed to be a one-week adventure in the wild became a year-long odyssey, in which my life nearly came to a swift end on countless occasions.

Inside the van I met a young German tourist who would be the only other voyager brave enough to take the expedition at that time. We had each hired a pair of Australian extreme outback experts who specialized in rugged and rough adventures in the Amazon and Guyana. The guides promised they would do their best to keep us safe, and then they detailed the longest list of life-threatening jungle realities that has ever been spoken. Anacondas, jaguars, giant spiders, giant bats, giant harpy eagles, caimans, bloodsucking insects of every variety, malaria, dangerously unpaved roads, and the legendary bushmaster viper.

Immediately after the Australians listed the countless ways *Mother Nature* might soon kill us, the German and I had to sign over our rights to sue if anything happened, and we had to list an emergency contact. Though a wise man may have turned back at this, I believed then, as I do now, that I could survive anything any other human has ever survived. And so, once again, I spun the *Wheel of Fortune,* and bet on the risks of adventure.

On the fourth day of that trip, my life changed forever. The four of us were traveling up a steep hill along a narrow stretch of unpaved road. Though the windowless jeep of the tour guides was sturdy enough, it was beyond its years and needed daily maintenance. I recall looking over the edge of the road, out onto a beautiful view of jungle and trees and azure sky. I thought I was the luckiest guy in the world, to be witnessing a view of the Amazon jungle that very few living humans had ever seen.

Suddenly the rear left wheel of the jeep slipped off the edge of the road. My quiet tranquility was immediately replaced with a storm of fear and adrenaline, for I felt immediately that the jolt from the slipping wheel was far stronger than the jeep's usual jostling. The driver's blond hair swung wildly as he tried to correct course, but it was to no avail. Before I could leap from the jeep to safety, the four of us fell down the side of the jungle cliff. I cannot remember what happened next, nor how I survived, but I would never see the Australian guides, the German tourist, or the windowless jeep again.

I awoke drenched, and lying on the banks of the Amazon River under the burning rays of the sun.

My entire body was bruised, my ribs felt fractured, I had large knots on both sides of my head, and I was missing my front teeth. After remembering my name and who I was, I began to drag myself from the river. Just as I was leaving the water, I saw an approaching ripple rise in the water 10 meters behind me. Aware of the threat of alligators and caiman in the area, I managed to muster up enough energy to rise and quickly enter the jungle.

I would go on to spend approximately forty four days alone in the jungle. Though I had read some books on wilderness survival to prepare for the trip, nothing could have prepared me for what I faced. I was always hungry, dehydrated, and swollen from mosquito bites. By day, I lived in constant fear and anxiety due to the non-stop orchestra of animal noises that surrounded me. At night, I seldom slept due to a reoccurring dream of the day of the crash. I knew that I was doomed if nothing changed, and I felt the life being drained from my body, as if by an evil spirit.

One day, I saw a gigantic and beautiful tree standing out above the other trees in the distance. I later learned that this was a kapok or silk cotton tree. It was thirty three meters tall and seven meters wide, and was like a giant compared to the trees which surrounded it. I walked for a day to get near it, and discovered that it was near a cliff and a waterfall. As I finally approached the tree, I saw the most beautiful array of fruits and flowers I had ever seen on a single tree. I soon became compelled by hunger to climb up the giant tree and gather some fruit to eat.

There were 7 different plateaus on the tree, like floors in a building, and the branches were covered in large thorns. I found some giant and delicious green fruit on the first plateau, and I stopped to fill my belly. The fruit was juicy and nutritious, and I cherished the meal and the liquids I then so desperately needed. Again, I felt like a lucky man, back on top of the Wheel of Fortune like a sphinx, and I suddenly felt an inner peace I had not felt since I the day I had awoken drenched on the banks of the Amazon River.

I looked higher up the tree and noticed a large bird's nest. Though I am a vegetarian, I debated the idea of eating the eggs, and killing unborn baby birds, because I had lost twenty -two pounds of weight. I finally decided that the protein from the eggs might prove essential to my survival, and so I climbed further up. When I arrived on the plateau of the nest, I discovered a newborn raptor and three of the largest eggs I had ever seen in my life. The newborn seemed blind, and was oblivious to me as I picked up one of its unborn siblings and weighed it in my *palm.*

As I contemplated how I was going to eat the eggs, I started having second thoughts as I watched the baby raptor. Though it was still helpless, it was already bubbling with a zest for life. Though I had every reason to think only of myself and my survival, the idea of cracking open one of those eggs started to become disgusting to me. Finally, though, I convinced myself that the universe had given me the eggs just as it had given me the fruits, as a gift for my long suffering.

As I went to smash two of the eggs together, the baby bird cried out faintly for the first time. This seeming coincidence was enough to make me pause to reconsider, and as I did, I noticed a flying black object in the far distance heading towards me. After a second, I realized that it was not a UFO, but in fact the mother of the birds. I immediately put the eggs back down and frantically began climbing down the tree, as I envisioned raptor talons tearing at my flesh. I was less than 10 feet from the ground when the harpy eagle finally reached the tree.

It circled its nest three times, then started towards me. I had paused my descent to watch the huge beast, and I could see that it was trying to time its attack. It continued circling the wide tree, and I lost sight of it. I then continued down quickly, and finally reached the ground. No more than a second after my feet hit the ground, the harpy flew past my face like lightening, and it slashed both my cheeks beneath my eyes. A few centimeters higher, and it would have blinded me. Fortunately, I escaped her with only scars.

I fell to my knees in agony, and I could barely open my eyes from the pain. Between my screams, I could hear the harpy swooping and screeching around me. I managed to rise to my feet, and as I ran blindly through the jungle, I could hear the harpy in violent pursuit. Every 13 seconds or so, there was a tremendous explosion of noise from it crashing through trees and branches and only narrowly missing me. I tripped and fell to the ground twelve times, and twelve times I successfully got up and continued my escape.

Just as I heard the raptor closing in behind me, I fell a 13th and final time. This time, I had unknowingly just come to the edge of the cliff near the waterfall. Once again, I fell and fell more, into a sea of green leaves and wooden branches. As I opened my eyes wide finally just after my foot did not land on solid ground, and I realized I was over the edge, I vividly recall my life flashing before my eyes.

When at last I awoke after this escape from death, I was lying in the modest hut of a Makushi medicine woman. My body was wrapped in fibrous bandages, and a pot of boiling liquid and herbs filled my room with a healing aroma. I had been rescued by three Makushi fishermen, and had been asleep for three days. I would recover in time, and go on to live with the Makushi until September of 2019. In time I would come face to face with all of the dangerous creatures the Australian tour guides had warned me about.

At first, though I was always treated civilly, many of the Makushi feared I was a 'keinaima', a type of evil, shape-shifting spirit that can transform into a human form. These keinaimas are said to bring chaos and death when they arrive to villages as strangers or outsiders.

They also attack lone individuals in the jungle who are separated from their group. My favorite keinaima fact was that they are reported to have the ability to create fireballs in the palms of their hands.

In time, the Makushi people grew to trust me, and I learned about their culture and myths. As I am fluent in all of the languages they speak except their native tongue, I became a language teacher for the community. In time, I began to court the young woman who was teaching me their native tongue. She was the daughter of the medicine-woman, and her name was Washaxa.

One day, whilst I was out foraging with Washaxa, she told me the story of the cave to the underworld. I had heard of tales of *Agartha* and *Shambhala* whilst studying the history of world myths, so I was very intrigued to learn more. She said the tale was probably just a myth, so no one had gone too far into the cave in several decades. Trying to impress her with my courage, I told her that I would venture into the cave all the way to the underworld, if she would but promise to kiss me when I returned. She smiled and agreed coyly, perhaps not realizing I was entirely serious.

I soon began to make preparations for my trip into the cave to the underworld. I was told it would take two weeks of voyaging underground before I reached the gates of the underworld, and I was told to expect several mysterious occurrences. It was explained to me that there would be edible fruits along the way before I got to the entrance to the underworld, so I did not need to pack much food.

Washaxa began to warn me against the trip, and her warnings grew ever more urgent as the date approached, until she even backed out of her promise to kiss me. Nevertheless, despite the circumstances which had led me to her village, my lust for adventures was still foolhardy and as strong as ever. She would eventually understand that my mind was made up, and finally she gave her blessings, and prayed I would be safe.

On the appointed day, Washaxa, her mother the medicine woman, and the tribe's Shaman walked with me for 10 hours to the entrance of the cave. After a protection ritual was performed over me by the shaman, and I thanked the medicine woman again for her kindness, I kissed Washaxa goodbye. I promised her that luck was on my side, and that I would return to her a hero, before I set off into the cave.

I walked for two days before I began to see the large open areas I had been told about. Vast underground plateaus so large they could fit entire football stadiums inside them. After another two days, I saw the large orbs of light which the Makushi had called underworld suns. The light was so bright that one could not look directly at them, but I could tell that they were balls of a plasma-like substance. There were even spatterings of grass and bushes, and beautiful flowers growing beneath the light of the plasma orbs.

It was not long after I passed the wind tunnel in which I was able to float that I came upon three large and very old vases. They were the same dull red color as the dirt and walls of that part of the cave, and were thus completely camouflaged. After I caught a glimmer of light from a piece of amethyst on one of the vases, I throw a rock in their direction in order to determine if something was moving. One of the vases shattered immediately, and as I got closer I could see that it was packed tight with papyri scrolls.

I could not understand the script, but I knew that it had to be an important discovery, and I recalled the discovery of the Dead Sea Scrolls. Again, I thanked the universe for my luck, and I began to stuff the scrolls in my bag. However, I did not have enough room for the scrolls and my food and supplies, for I had not planned on bringing back anything. I decided then and there to end my voyage to the underworld. I had found something undoubtedly important, and so I convinced myself that a trip to the underworld could wait.

I returned to the surface world and the village, and then I returned to Georgetown, Guyana a month after that. I would later learn that the scrolls were written in both *Medu Neter* – Egyptian Hieroglyphics – and the *Proto-Sinaitic* script, also known as *Early Alphabet*. This is the most ancient script discovered to date, and it has been found on cave walls throughout the world. Being a lover of all things Ancient Egyptian, I decided to learn how to translate the papyri myself, so that I could present the wisdom of the scrolls to the world.

I returned to America just before COVID-19 shut the world down in 2020, and for the last few years I have been decoding the story that unfolds in those papyri. What I discovered in those scrolls has forever changed me, and I can no longer go on living my life as I had been doing. The scrolls recount the myth of Krstjah Rastari, the world's first internationally recognized mythical hero, avatar, and christ figure. It is now my honest belief that there was once a one world culture and spiritual system that was based around the 'million-year-old myth' of Krstjah Sa Ra Rastari, the heroic and advented son of the sun.

I believe that it is from the legacy of the myth of Krstjah that history created Gilgamesh, Osiris and Heru, Dionysus and Hercules and Perseus, Enoch, Jesus of Nazareth, Buddha, Krishna, Superman, Thor, and every godlike hero and religious idol ever conceived. For as I got deeper into the story written on those papyri, I saw exact similarities between Krstjah and all these figures. In fact, the teachings of Krstjah are as if one syncretically combined the teachings of all the major spiritual systems, for his words are essentially the same as those reportedly said by the saints and saviors of every major spiritual tradition.

The parallels to our current world in the myth of Krstjah were easy and obvious to see, so I have taken some poetic liberty of updating the myth for my modern audience. However, I have continued the timeframe of the saga, which is anachronistic. Like a dream, the story spans thousands of years, yet everything seems to happen all at once.

I am convinced of the authenticity of the underlying message of the Rastari myth: that every soul may achieve spiritual immortality through a heroic journey of personal evolution, redemption, and sanctification, and through the I AM awareness that we are all a part of the one Almighty god.

I am also convinced of the vital role of shared cultural myths and symbols in building lasting communities. My nation, America, is currently fracturing in every radical way imaginable, and the only glue that held us together – pop culture – is falling apart in the wake of the revelations of Hollywood's corruption.

As the most modern science of today finally admits that it was wrong to outright reject the wisdom of the ancient shamans and mystics, I propose we rediscover the truth of mysticism and magic and spirituality, the truth which not only held nations together for millenniums, but also built megalithic structures that still stand until this very day.

I am now a practicing devotee of the Magical Order of Rastari, and I welcome others to join me in accessing the transcendental ecstasy brought to our world more than twenty-five thousand years ago with the saga of Krstjah Rastari.

May these testaments become for the 21st century and the Age of Aquarius our new sublime, divine, and mythical. Let Krstjah Sa Ra Rastari become again our heroic model and idol, for it is he that is the Ganymede pouring down the milk and honey of transcendence in the Aquarius constellation. It is Krstjah which speaks to us through our hearts, and it is he that watches over us from Sirius.

Surround yourself with FRIENDS if possible, and together read of Krstjah's pastimes and legends and miraculous magic. Meditate on the meaning of the symbols, and seriously consider the words of Krstjah. Be inspired to find your own angel and spiritual guide, your own Iyrin and Neter. Have Faith, be strong and resilient in the face of your challenges, and become the true Super-Heru version of yourself!

Heru Krstjah, Heru Krstjah,
Krstjah Krstjah, Heru Heru.
Heru Rastar, Heru Rastar,
Rastar Rastar, Heru Heru.
Axé!

Twilight

Axé!
All praises and honor due to the Almighty, to the I in I,
and to the light of this world, Lord Krstjah Sa Ra Rastari,
Son of the sun, hero and savior, emperor and mighty king,
Ever living in our hearts and on Sirius, forever let thy name ring.
Forever protect the righteous and those that know and love thee
Forever let our path towards Herudom be free.
Selah!

Axé! My heart overflows with delight and wonder, for mine eyes have witnessed the glory of the Almighty, and I in I here give my testament and testimony. I in I witnessed the exemplar life and miraculous works of the supreme avatar of the Almighty. Yes, I, Saint Guanyin Sattvastar, walked side by side with the Sun of Man, Lord Krstjah Sa Ra Rastari, as he journeyed across the world.

I in I watched him save the world and us all, not once, not twice, but thrice, all with the grace and beauty of a dancer's twirl. For Lord Krstjah Rastari is the archetype, the paragon, the perfect person who was divinity made flesh, advented for our salvation.

Krstjah was given the oil of the gods, born of celestial sun through a righteous womb, and he has saved you and I from the necessity of reincarnation. Lord Krstjah Rastari became enlightened in front of mine very eyes, and I in I saw him come to know the Neter which liveth within even you and I.

Krstjah awoke the I Am awareness and became more than he ever imagined, and I in I here recount his epic legacy for the exaltation and glorification of the I.

Before the creation, there was only the I, the all-mighty One and creator which is an unknowable and ineffable deity that is All. We can never truly understand or even imagine the mystery of the I, so it is our custom to symbolize the I as a crystal ball.

The I is all powerful, all present, all knowing, all good, all of being and all of becoming, all powerful, and thus we call it Almighty. The I is everything and nothing, inside and beyond space and time, a part of us yet greater, what was, what is, what will and what might be.

In the first and last dimension in a field of infinite white light at the center of the heart of everything yet wholly out of sight. Some refer to this 13th dimension of the I as Heaven or Jannah or Moksha or Nirvana, yet we Rastarists call it *Delight*.

For its own prerogative, the Almighty decided to remember every possibility as an actuality, and to know again all that is the I. To re-experience everything in itself once again, the I dreamt a simulation to sift through every what, when, where, and why.

And so, the Almighty suspended its disbelief and closed its eyes and its intention and intelligence and intuition, for a duration of time. This simulation and dream formed in a new and empty dimension called the Holy Spirit inside of the Almighty's spirit and mind.

Hidden there in the Holy Spirit were three eternal aspects of the Almighty, aspects which were intertwined, sublime, and divine. We call these aspects Principals and Omnicestors, and they are the symbols of the Almighty's consciousness, power, and mind.

The trinity of Akasha Kibo the Dweller, Shekinga Shira the Creator, and Jewhuti Maat Mawenzi the Architect. Akasha Kibo is the omnipresent consciousness of the Almighty, the unseen watcher who has seen it all, and will see what is next.

We symbolize Akasha as a body as big as a planet, with skin made from the stars and the vast blackness of space. Akasha is the silent dweller that is inside and surrounding all things, a constant companion and camera, with only a shadow's face.

Shekinga Shira is the omnipotent powers of the Almighty, the generating and manifesting magic that is the great mother. Shekinga is the imagination of the Almighty's dreaming mind, the Principal of creation, and the power that rules over all others.

We symbolize Shekinga Shira as a head as big as a planet, and each of the four sides of the head show a hooded and veiled face. Beneath the veils are the faces of a female child, a male, a woman, and an old man, and Shekinga's starry skin is also as dark as space.

Jewhuti Maat Mawenzi, the Architect, is the growing bank of wisdom of the Almighty in the Holy Spirit, and is omniscient. Jewhuti is all knowledge and wisdom, and the expression of the Will of the Almighty, so we Rastarists also call Jewhuti 'IT.'

IT analyzes the unfolding of Shekinga's creation by reviewing the records of Akasha with attentive titillation. IT is the symbol and source of truth, order, balance, harmony, reciprocity, justice, righteousness, revelation, and divination. We symbolize Jewhuti Mawenzi as a giant priest with the head of a black raven with golden eyeballs and pupils. He bears a golden third eye and wears turquoise robes, and he learns and teaches as he transcribes in the Book of All for us, his pupils.

Before the beginning of space and time in the Holy Spirit, IT was still asleep, Shekinga had not yet created, and Akasha was still blind. Though Akasha could not see, it was conscious of its own existence, and when it stirred from anxiety, Shekinga created time.

From the crown chakra of Shekinga's head arose a lotus flower, and when it blossomed, a clear egg sat at the center of its whorls. IT was awakened and Akasha could now see this new dimension, a translucent ball which shimmered like a crystal pearl. Akasha watched as Shekinga then created the first everlasting Inicestor inside of the ball, the Principal of Time called Ihah Eternity. And in no time at all, the ball expanded exponentially as Shekinga simultaneously created the Principal of Space called Ihum Infinity.

Ihah is the great black snake of chaos and infinite possibility, a snake so massive it swallows all of space and even its own tail. Inside of the ouroboros' belly is the ever expanding Ihum, all spaces and every place, and symbolized as a great Mysticeti whale.

Inside of Ihum's mouth is None, an infinite and dark ocean which contains all of the space and energy possible in Ihum Infinity. Vibrating at the fastest frequency yet seemingly still, None is like the blackness of our calm minds when we are filled with serenity. Above None is a sky filled with a fog of spiritual cloudy ether and other forms of negatively charged spiritual energy. In time some of the energy becomes ether, and some of the ether becomes energy, and correspondences arise from this synergy.

In time, corresponding ripples of vibration began to dance in unison, and this created Irie Rajas, the Principal of Rhythm. As Irie formed in None, a second principal called Ites Rajas formed simultaneously in the ether to balance the schism.

Symbolically, Irie Rajas is a massive silver dragon that creates rhythmic waves and ripples across the ocean of None. And Ites is symbolized as a gigantic thick-billed murre made of ether which trails its twin Irie as if it has it on the run.

In the unfoldment of time, Inicestor Irie Rajas immaculately conceived an egg, the Egg of Adom and the seed of matter. Ites witnessed the birth of this crystal egg, and when the egg started to sink down, Ites dived into None and chased after. Ites pursued the Egg of Adom, the root of our universe, as it swiftly fell deeper and deeper still into the chaotic ocean. With every passing moment Ites swam faster into the abyss, completely free of fear, for that was still then an unformed notion.

Only after Ites finally began traveling faster than the speed of spiritual light, did Ites at last reach and then swallow Adom. Just as the egg entered its mouth, Ites transformed into a blue winged dragon, the Principal of our Universe, Inicestor Ion.

Ion swam up through the spiritual energy of None to its surface, and then opened its mouth to reveal the egg still on its tongue. Irie Rajas witnessed again its egg, and after she intertwined her body with Ion's, the two swayed in union as if dancing to a song. In the harmony of their feminine and masculine energies, Ion and Irie ignited the soul of Adom, and it began to shine like a sun. Now running on both spiritual energy and physical electromagnetic energy, Adom transformed into the globe of our universe, Zion.

Zion has seven planes of existence, and the lowest plane is the dark and boiling ocean that cleanses the karma of spirits, called the Deep. In the center of the Deep grows a magnificent red, white, and golden lotus flower, and all of the higher planes of Zion rest on its peak.

Resting on the lotus petals is Aghora, the spiritual underworld which dead souls voyage through until their time of judgment arrives. Above Aghora is Agartha, a physical underworld of precious minerals and pristine waters where the elect live thousand-year lives. In the center of Agartha stands a tower of obsidian that never ends, and our plane and planet, Kismet, is the tower's pyramidion. An underground plane of caves is beneath our feet, and at the center of this planet is the great Mt. Meru, the true prime meridian.

Mt. Meru is on the island of Atlantis at Kismet's center, and at Meru's base is a gate to the underworld and the great Tree of Life. Above the sky is the Celestial Sea of stars and planets, and above that is Shambhala, home of the Celestials and their after-lives.

There in Shambhala the castles and gardens and seven heavens of the Principals are spread out along an Elysian countryside. For the Deep is the reward for souls judged iniquitous, and Shambhala is the reward and paradise where righteous souls reside. At the center of Shambhala is the golden palace of Kairos Ra Stari, the Lord of Kismet and Shambhala, and the Principal of the Sun. The golden palace and heaven of Kairos Ra Stari stretches from the bottom to the top of Shambhala, ending with a door out from Zion.

From the start of eternity, Jewhuti Maat Mawenzi could see that every plane of existence existed in an unfoldment of three. Like father, mother, and child, or dweller, creator, and thinker, Jewhuti understood that there is always on some level a trinity. Jewhuti then gave names to the Omnicestors, and to the Inicestors, and then IT began to closely analyze the product of Irie and Ites. In time, IT understood the planes of Zion, and IT understood that what occurs on Kismet corresponds to the influences of the stars' light.

In time, as IT understood the stars, Shekinga began to create bodies, called suns and planets, which could embody the stars' energies. And so the Sun formed to embody the courage given by starlight, and the Moon was created to embody the stars' nourishing serenity.

Shekinga had created personified souls for every sun and planet which she created, and every planet is a Principal now. Our planet Kismet is the dog-headed guardian angel Shai, the Principal of faith and destiny, and he symbolizes hard work and rides a plow. Jupiter is Besti, the jovial Principal of luck, Mars is Sekkemi, the lioness of strength, and Mercury is Hapi, the joyful musician. The Inicestors were given planets in Zion as well, and Ihum resides over Neptune, Ion over Uranus, and from Venus IT watches and listens.

In the beginning of Kismet, the Principal of Saturn and temperance, named Asaraset, was as hot and powerful as Kairos Ra Stari. In time, Asaraset judged Kairos egotistical, and he waged war against Kairos for the hand of the Moon, Iyah Stari. Their fiery war ravished the lifeless planet for a million years, until Shai Royg Bivi asked IT to end the war and save Kismet. IT judged against Asaraset, so Shekinga diminished Saturn's influence, and then created the sun-moon of Agartha, called Rahu, for Asaraset.

To this day, Asaraset in the form of Rahu leaves the underworld and voyages up to this planet on several annual trips. Although we cannot see Rahu directly at those times, we can see its shadow, and so are reminded of Asaraset's power during every eclipse.

With time under just one sun, the raging fire ceased, and the face of Kismet cooled to a mineral rich, bubbling still. In time, Shekinga created life and living souls from bits of Shai's divine soul, and Shekinga made this life according to IT's will.

In more time still, Shekinga created original and independent souls from the residue of ether which remained in the ionosphere. Shekinga generated life according to harmonious and sacred geometry, and she gave life the ability to survive and persevere. Shekinga created microbes, and then plants, trees, fungi, insects, and finally animals with self-awareness came to be. At every stage of the evolution of life, waters were the place of creation, thus new forms of life always got their start in the seas.

Before history began, Kismet unfolded as above so below, and life behaved according to the energies of the Celestial Principals. As Shai Rogue Bivi is the very ground and stage where the adventure of life unfolds, its sway over the course of history is essential. Shai, and the planet itself, is tidal in its power, mountainous in its grandeur, at times simply seismic and at others volcanic. Shai is the source of our very flesh and bones, and by living in our shadows, Shai is the guardian angel of all things organic.

The Celestial Principals realized their influence paled in comparison to Shai's, and they cried out for equal power over fate. Shekinga then made souls with consciousness, sentient beings which the Celestials could not only influence but even infiltrate.

Through possession of conscious beings, the Celestials could briefly walk the planet as they experienced mortal life and sensations. The Celestials would delight in their living avatars, then watch the being from on high and observe the consequences of their visitations. Yet the Celestials realized that they could not alter the destiny of beings with these short visits, so they searched for better solutions. Soon they learned they could possess the bodies of some pure souls without end, thanks to psychic abilities in their constitutions.

As the Celestials lived out entire mortal lives in the bodies of pure souls, some of them by chance impregnated the mothers' of new pure souls. This soon gave the Celestials demigod bodies to play with and live in, and a period of legendary events began to unfold.

This was the *Age of the Avatars*, the thousand years when supernatural living beings of every species appeared on Kismet. There were fantastic creatures with unimaginable powers, and the so-called angels and monsters of every myth, legend, and epic.

There are two categories of demigod avatars, the good ones and the bad ones, and those which aided others are called the Iyrin. The avatars which selfishly pursued their own ends and in doing so wreaked havoc and destruction on others are called the Jinn. In time, the influence and consequences of the Jinns grew out of balance, for their selfish recklessness was inspiration to the wicked. Through the conspiracy and secret organization of the Jinns and the iniquitous, the Iyrin were overpowered and Kismet became afflicted.

Soon after even the mightiest of all heroes and Iyrins were defeated, a century of endless war and iniquity nearly destroyed Kismet. Detonated nuclear bombs and weapons of mass destruction unleashed the World Flood which cleansed the planet and climate. The Celestials understood that they were responsible for this calamity, so they repented and prayed for the planet's resurrection. The Omnicestors worked together to restore the ecosphere and restart life, and the world returned to its natural perfection.

Jewhuti forbade the Celestials from ever again creating avatars, and though most were in agreement, Asaraset required recognition. Asaraset said that as he had never spawned a Jinn, he should now be king, yet he was speaking not from reason but ambition.

For Asaraset's tower had become a magnet and a bank for the dark etheric energy which was created from the karma and sin of the Jinn. This karma should have been cleansed by the Deep, yet it remained because the immortal Principals were responsible for the sin. This dark energy had imbalanced Asaraset, so he claimed that only he, as king, could save Kismet from another invasion of Jinn. Jewhuti Mawenzi praised Asaraset's temperance, and Shekinga gave Saturn its rings, yet IT rejected Asaraset's request, to his chagrin.

The Age of the Avatars was no more, yet their memory lives on in the myths and legends of superheroes and mutants and demons. And these memories would begin to take on a life of their own when enough sentient beings shared the same concept while dreaming.

In time, the black cloud surrounding Asaraset's tower fed the seeds of imbalance in him, and this began an inner upheaval. When these seeds finally germinated into their unnatural flower, a spirit of selfishness awoke in him and became a spirit of evil. This unbalanced spirit of evil in Asaraset suddenly began to attract and absorb some of the dark ether that surrounded the tower. Asaraset's spirit was overwhelmed by the influx of negative energy, and it was forced to split in two to contain the energy and power.

And in no time, Asaraset stood before his opposite, Tessarasa, the embodiment of his shadow and the very Principal of evil. Tessarasa's face is a white mask fixed in an unholy grin, and he is the god of selfishness and debauchery, and the enemy of all people.

Asaraset was purified of the negativity long within him, and he seemed fully liberated from a terrible, hypnotic spell. Tessarasa sprang into being fully self-conscious, and it rejoiced and danced like a guilty prisoner accidentally freed from its cell.

Tessarasa began to gloat of its self-creation, and claimed that it could help Asaraset regain his power and become the king of Shambhala. Asaraset did not hesitate, for he instantly understood the evil nature of Tessarasa, and he leapt at Tessarasa with the force of an impala. Asaraset's double-headed Scythe had also split, so Tessarasa met Asaraset's Scythe of Doom with the Scythe of Fate in his hands. And so, the preamble to the advent of the Sun of Man was at its end, and the epic of Krstjah Sa Ra Rastari truly began.

The ensuing battle between Asaraset and Tessarasa was like an epic clash between matter and anti-matter, and it shook the Tower. Finally, Tessarasa got the space he needed to rotate his Scythe in a circle as Asaraset watched, and this activated the Scythe's hidden power.

Asaraset was now totally hypnotized, and in the world of his illusion, he finally landed a serious blow against the Evil One. As he approached Tessarasa, and it begged for its life, the real Tessarasa approached the motionless Asaraset, knowing he had won. When Tessarasa was near Asaraset, he absorbed more of the dark ether, and manifested a long black snake from his sacral plexus. When the snake bit Asaraset, Asaraset involuntarily decapitated it, as the snake's ice venom flowed throughout his nexus.

As Tessarasa writhed in agony from this wound, Asaraset collapsed to the tower's floor, just as he slew what was only an illusion. Asaraset woke up from the dream of the Scythe of Fate only to realize he had been duped and was paralyzed by the ether's suffusion. The dark ether flowed into Tessarasa and it began to regenerate him, until he was caressing his snake's new, disfigured head. Tessarasa then used the dark ether to reconfigure the floor of the Tower, and he created an obsidian tomb to act as Asaraset's bed.

The disjointed snake head also fed on the dark ether from the floor, and it reversed both death and 'lived,' and became the first 'devil.' It became Apothis, the black floating snake, and it was both the first horseman of Tessarasa, and the first to see the Demiurge revel.

Tessarasa vowed to exterminate all sentient beings, in order to prevent them from destroying Xibalba, his name for the underworld. He created a plan to use unjudged souls in an army of the dead, and he wanted a human avatar to be the apocalypse's herald. Tessarasa created a forbidden Jinn so that it could live in our physical world, and this Jinn was called Tesarak Iset.

The avatar Iset was gifted with the idi and psychic ability of *Telepathy*, and became the king of Romilon and then emperor of Kismet. He had eyes that shone an eerie and icy blue, dark hair and pale skin, and though he was no giant, he was bigger than normal men. Emperor Iset's idi could increase the power of another's shadows and selfishness, and he traveled the world turning kings to sin.

In time, Jewhuti Maat Mawenzi began to closely analyze the Akashic Records, the recordings of Akasha, and IT saw all of Tesarak Iset. In time, IT understood that the life of Tesarak was unnatural, and that Iset was an avatar, and Jewhuti assumed it was Asaraset.

Jewhuti then delved deeper into the hidden and dark mind of Emperor Iset, and in no time it found the spirit of the Evil One. Tessarasa immediately fled Iset's body and flew to Xibalba, for the light of Jewhuti's third eye awareness is as powerful as the sun. Jewhuti chased after Tessarasa, yet the Evil One managed to enter what it now called the Babel Tower, its impenetrable sanctuary. Jewhuti as the black and gold raven could not penetrate the clouds of dark ether, so IT went off to formulate a solution to the Adversary.

Though Tessarasa fled the mortal body of Emperor Tesarak Iset, the oil of the Evil One had remained in his jewels. As Jewhuti was chasing the Demiurge to Xibalba, Emperor Iset impregnated the unholy virgin appointed to bear Tessarasa's spool. Tessarasa had failed to create the next demigod avatar for himself, but this union still managed to spawn a Demijinn named Kathol Iset. Kathol Iset would grow up and eventually become the new emperor, yet he was but a pawn whose true role was only to abet.

Though he was not a Jinn or full demigod, Kathol Iset also had magical idis, and he inherited Tessarasa's twisted will. Tessarasa would eventually command Kathol through the Ark of Tesarak, ensuring that his demijinn would remain the dark mill.

Before the mortal Tesarak Iset died, he also fled to the underworld, and he took with him Waor and Lyes, his most brutal guards. They were all met at the gate to the underworld by a gigantic Apothis, and on its back they were flown to the Tower's courtyard. When at last they began to penetrate the black clouds of dark ether, they screamed in agony as their flesh was reconfigured. They screamed as if they were in a lava pit, and in no short time they had been turned into monsters and transfigured.

Tesarak had become Shaytan, the goat-man in red armor, Waor was now a bony grim reaper, and Lyes had grown spider limbs in the distortion. Now transformed, they entered Babel and met Tessarasa, whose footstool was the tomb of Asaraset, and he met his Four Horsemen.

And thus was the twilight of Kismet, when Ion the Superself of our universe lamented. And so, at last, our hero Lord Krstjah Sa Ra Rastari was to be advented.

Nativity

Axé!
All praises and honor due to the Almighty, to the I in I,
and to the light of this world, Lord Krstjah Sa Ra Rastari,
Son of the sun, hero and savior, emperor and mighty king,
Ever living in our hearts and on Sirius, forever let thy name ring.
Forever protect the righteous and those that know and love thee
Forever let our path towards Herudom be free.
Selah!

Jewhuti Maat Mawenzi returned to Shambhala, and he convened the Celestial Principals to his dazzling crystal palace. The dome palace of Jewhuti is the jewel of Heaven, for it sparkles as if a diamond snow globe which contains an aurora borealis.

When all 11 Celestials were gathered around Jewhuti's throne, IT ordained that they all had a role to play in freeing Asaraset. Each of the Celestials gave a drop of their spiritual essence to the holy oil IT would use to anoint an avatar and savior of Kismet.

IT then sent out ravens to search the world, and find the perfect righteous mother for he who would become Krstjah. The Celestials once again had a soul of their own to watch, so they waited for the day they heard a raven say *Hallelujah*!

The ravens of Jewhuti became flesh and they flew across Kismet, and the squawks of their ancestors can be heard to this day. The ravens searched every continent and country, every city and county, and they infiltrated the local bird array.

Kismet was then still a beautiful and bountiful world, and we humans could still live until the age of 365. It was a world of cultural and religious and spiritual diversity, where the unique Faith of a community could grow and thrive. The scientific evidence for Faith was well-acknowledged, so even babes knew of the spirits that cannot be seen with the eye. In Kismet, the Spiritists had replaced the scientists and priests, so for every question, some god or spirit was the reason why.

In the years before our Lord, every nation of Kismet was ruled according to its own system, so there were democracies and kings. Every nation was a part of the Global Imperial Court, with the most powerful nations at the head, and others in its wings.

The GIC was headed by the Emperor, who was usually the head of the most powerful nation at the time of the annual vote. But after Tesarak Iset became emperor, the nation of Romilon and the devilish kings it empowered took the GIC by the throat. Kathol Iset was named the emperor at only 13, and he continued his father's spread of inequity from the highest places. It was in this age of Romilon's spread of 'demijinnocracy' that the beauty of the world had begun to be destroyed by disgraces.

The Isets routinely ruined nations by first destroying their leaders and then, in the ensuing chaos, they brought to power wicked puppets. Of the nations which remained righteous and free before Krstjah's advention, the nation of Nubitopia shone as if a precious nugget.

There lived in Nubitopia a beautiful princess and a world famous Spiritist named Queen Omega Negustiti Rastari. Queen Omega was world-renowned as a spiritual singer, and it was well known she was a virgin married to the I. Her chastity only increased her charm, for Queen Omega was one of the most beautiful women in the history of Kismet. She was blessed with a divine smile, luxurious locks, dazzling eyes, succulent skin, and a legendary body of assets.

Queen Omega catalyzed love and joy and spiritual ecstasy across the world wherever she performed and graced her presence. Her body drove men wild with desire, and though she was courted by the world's wealthiest men, only the I in I was her pleasance. Queen Omega toured the world for one hundred years, performing songs which taught the Faith of Nubitopia, the Faith in the Almighty. Queen Omega Negustiti Rastari's life was epic in and of itself, for she was a superstar Spiritist, as if 'the Rastari Aphrodite.'

When Queen Omega had reached the age of 130, she became enlightened and reached the stage of a buddha. It was then, on a starry night in the fourth lunar month, that from her windowsill the Principals heard a raven cry Hallelujah!

That night, as Queen Omega slept, she began to lucid dream, for she knew very well how to remain conscious in the astral dimension. In that space-time of dreams and the imagination, the spiritually adept move around freely to advance their ascension. In the astral realm, Queen Omega as a babe rode Shai as a winged dog around the Celestial Sea, and she saw faces on each planet. She saw Sekkemi on Mars, Hapi on Mercury, and so forth, and finally she reasoned she was in a vision, and tried to understand it.

After she circled Kairos the sun, she was transported to a valley surrounded by hills under a star drenched, super moon sky. Every one of Jewhuti's 144,000 ravens was there, sitting atop the hills as silhouettes, as Queen Omega heard her future son's thunderous cry.

Queen Omega turned and finally beheld the awe-inspiring visage of the supreme avatar, baby Krstjah Sa Ra Rastari. His skin shone as dark as night, and his eyes, hair, and lips were as gold as sunlight, and only his smile has been seen by living eyes. Baby Krstjah wore a golden prince crown, golden silk pants, a fiery halo surrounded his head, and his cry resounded as thunder. A blue glow shone just before his movements, and a red glow lingered just after, and he had a golden flute which he stared at in wonder.

Queen Omega and Krstjah locked eyes, and his visage filled her with transcendental bliss, and she knew the exhilarating love of

Krstjah. Krstjah smiled at his mother, and when he tried to stand to go to her, he instead began to levitate, then age, and then he became a star.

The star of Krstjah rose high into the sky, and though its intense light was blinding Queen Omega, she could not look away. Tremendous wind and air began to fly from the star of Krstjah, and the ravens circled the star until they made a giant affray. The cloud of the ravens then merged into the black star of Krstjah, making it grow much larger and brighter ever still. Then a raven's feather emerged from the star of Krstjah, and the Holy Oil of the Celestials poured down through its quill.

The gleaming, glistening, milky white waterfall of smoky spiritual light bathed Queen Omega and the ground where she stood. Queen Omega felt the most thrilling and amorous sensations she had ever experienced emanating from her womanhood. Flowers and herbs sprang forth and blossomed under the light, as Queen Omega began tearing off her clothes in ecstasy. As the waterfall came to an end, the light lit fire to the flowers and herbs, and this created an intoxicating fragrance medley.

The scents and aromas immediately calmed Queen Omega, and she breathed in deeply as she sat down gracefully into *padmasana*. A cold breeze swept down into the valley, and as it swirled, it cooled and baptized Queen Omega as she reached true *Nirvana*. She then heard a wise voice say, "Beloved Queen Omega, the spirit and fire of the highest Principals now rests within thy womb. From thy pure matrix shall soon come forth the son of the sun to break the seals on righteousness' tomb."

Queen Omega opened her eyes, and was back in her bed in Nubitopia, where she saw the raven of Jewhuti watching over her still. She recognized the raven from her vision and realized she had had more than a vision as the raven turned on the windowsill. The raven, named Crovin, then flew to a nearby tree, destined to forever watch vigilantly over the one that had been KRST and anointed. Queen

Omega then knew that she was pregnant with the Sa Ra, and she sang thanksgivings to the Almighty for being so appointed.

I n the years before our Lord, it was customary across Kismet for newborn royalty to receive a forecast of their destiny from Spiritists. The most skilled Spiritists, including Queen Omega, had mastered numerology and astrology as if they were astrophysicists.

Kathol Iset's forecast foretold him becoming the most powerful man in history, but he would be decapitated by progeny of the gods. So when the greedy emperor was not scheming for more gold and power, he was obsessed with killing his nemesis despite all odds. Emperor Iset employed thousands of dark Spiritists and spies and assassins, whose duty was to find and destroy all potential threats. Any one across the world who was rumored to be divine or supernatural in any way was to be murdered with no regrets.

In a world of Faith such as Kismet, miracles and magic were as commonplace as rainbows and resplendently hued sunsets. Most of these alleged miracles were mere fantasies or fabrications, and the Spiritist's duty of confirming true magic was their chief asset. Claims of *immaculate conception* were the easiest to refute, for a second source of human DNA could always be identified. After the investigation of the world's top Spiritist confirmed the miracle of Queen Omega's child, the people of Kismet were beatified.

But the first person to receive this confirmation, Emperor Iset, meet the news with goosebumps, a cold sweat, and the intent to kill. Not once in two thousand years had an immaculate conception been confirmed, so he was certain this might be the real deal.

Nubitopia was a free country, completely uncorrupted and uninfiltrated by the spies and forces of Romilon and Emperor Iset. Iset reasoned that he would only be able to kill Queen Omega if he created his grandest of schemes, and employed all his evil magic.

Iset continued to scheme as he watched Queen Omega on his television, on a global newscast that was broadcasted across Kismet. Queen Omega was then living in a palatial estate near the palace, and in its marvelous gazebo she hosted superstar duets. Famous performers and Spiritists sang together in front of the Nubitopians allowed to the castle grounds for the occasion. Queen Omega's pregnancy became a righteous spiritual spectacle, and peoples of all Faiths sojourned to Nubitopia to give her veneration.

Emperor Iset convened the heads of Romilon's Faith, and they began the bloody rituals which were a part of the Faith's secret rites. They began to torture and sacrifice a pure infant of a different species for 165 consecutive nights. And then, from through the wires of the cathedral style radio of the Ark of Tessarasa, pored forth Iset's gift from the Evil One. The dark poison of Apothis seeped out, and every priest which helped collect it died only 13 minutes after the deed was done.

Iset now had his weapon and its antidote, but he knew that it would not be easy to poison the highly guarded expectant mother. Queen Omega was well aware of the grim fate of the allegedly miraculous in that age, and she had guarded herself from becoming another.

Whilst most of the world only watched the daily pregnancy ceremonies, wealthy suitors privately met with Queen Omega. Any royal suitors who paid seven figures might have a private audience with her, so Nubitopia became as if the first Geneva. Emperor Iset owned more gold and money than any man in history, so he planned on poisoning Queen Omega whilst in disguise. Iset then stole the identity of the king of a small island which he had colonized and plundered after the king had met his demise.

Iset paid the Rastari family not seven but 11 figures for private time with Queen Omega, her doula, and her elite bodyguards. On a solstice day, in a beautiful courtyard away from the crowds, was where the masked Iset began to play his evil house of cards.

Iset lied through his teeth, saying that it was his destiny to be with Queen Omega, and that he had forsaken all of his wives. Queen Omega could sense his evil intent, despite his hypnosis, for she felt each of his words like the sharp tips of knives. When she refused his proposal, Iset began to claim that his country had a prophecy that detailed the return of their god. Iset said that the head Spiritist of his Faith was certain their god was Omega's child, and he brought out charts and props for this charade.

Iset promised that Krstjah was thus destined to be the greatest of all kings, with a thousand-year legacy and a golden monument atop a volcano. Iset pretended to be surprised, yet it was but another stage of his plan, when Queen Omega thanked him and then said no.

Iset thanked Queen Omega for her time, and let florid lies about his hope for her health spill from his devilish lips and tongue. *Long live the Prince*! and other such fallacious exultations he sang, before prepping the special gift for Queen Omega he had brung. One of his assassins, able to transform their faces beyond disguise, brought out the poison in two emerald chalices on a silver platter. The assassin now had the face of the real server, for Iset had bribed one of Omega's guards for all intel on the matter.

Iset swore the drink was the specialty of his nation, and that it would bestow long life and great intelligence upon the child in her womb. The assassin tested the potion, and when she approved of its safety, Queen Omega picked up what was the chalice of her doom. The assassin's mouth and stomach had been lined with metal so as to not let the poison affect them before the plot took root. Iset promised the assassin she would be taken out of the country and paid that night, but nothing could have been further from the truth.

After Queen Omega had swallowed the poison, Iset bid her adieu, and sped away to consume the antidote the Evil One had made. Iset was out of the country, and the fake guard had slipped off and died, all before the health of Queen Omega began to fade. Before the eyes of the gathered crowd, after Queen Omega stood up and nearly fainted, she was rushed to the castle's healing center. Whilst the world waited for any news and watched the center, for fear of spies, only the most renowned healers could enter.

After the dead guard's body had been found, all of the healers were alerted that Queen Omega had been poisoned by a deadly brew. The Spiritists worked all night to heal Queen Omega, and after praying through the night, the faithful were bathed by a morning dew. With the sun came the news, Queen Omega and Krstjah were alive and well, and the world rejoiced anew for the coming birth. But they then learned that Queen Omega was now blind and deaf, and that her days were numbered on this earth.

The joyous festivities would continue without Queen Omega, for she was hidden in secret chambers for her last days on Kismet. And in but a few weeks more, the waters of Queen Omega broke open, and thus began the birth of the almighty infant.

On that glorious and august day, the sun became solstice again, and Queen Omega stood in a private pool under the open sky. Gathered were all of the angelic Iyrins and consorts of the Principals, the holiest Spiritists of Kismet, and the members of Rastari.

The Spiritists bore witness to the array of spiritual watchers there, and the Rastari family bore witness to two supernatural events. At the moment Krstjah left Queen Omega's body, a strong breeze burst forth, and it was filled with an enchanting scent. This breeze was a wave of purifying, magnetic energy, and it brought an involuntary smile to the face of everyone it reached. And, when Krstjah was raised out of the waters, his first cry seemed to come from the sky, arising as if a clap of thunder unleashed.

Queen Omega instantly felt both the joy of accomplishing her *Toll for Immortality* and the agonizing pain of the poison and her doom. As she sat down in the water, her third eye fully opened and she could see Kairos Ra Stari and Jewhuti Maat Mawenzi that noon. Through this hidden light, she saw all humans there gathered in angelic, Iyrin form, and she saw every wonderful spirit there in the sky. Yet she had never seen such transcendent and profound beauty as her new child Krstjah, and he never again left her third eye.

Queen Omega grabbed hold of Krstjah, and felt a surge of energy flowing into her body as if plasma was charging her electrons. Placing Krstjah onto her bosom filled her with an ecstatic joy and bliss, and love beyond all imagination and every spectrum.

Krstjah's skin seemed as hot as the sun, yet it did not burn Queen Omega, and she praised the Almighty for giving birth to the Sa Ra. Though she was being paralyzed by Apothis' poison, she held Krstjah above her head, so that she may see him shine again as a star.

As she held Krstjah up, Queen Omega knew her last breath was in her lungs, and the fear of losing the love of Krstjah overcame her. Queen Omega whispered an ancient and magical Rastari phrase into Krstjah's ears, and then she asked to become Krstjah's retainer. "Almighty, I in I give thanks for the duty of keeping clean and compassionate the heart of my son, Krstjah, while he lives in flesh." At that, Queen Omega's soul forever left her heart and body, and it entered Krstjah's heart, where it could now nurture him afresh.

With his mother's soul now in his heart, baby Krstjah received her insight, and now understood all she had understood and taught. Her wisdom swirled around in his newborn mind like a tempest of smoke, and when he had a question, it would become a solid thought. Krstjah knew the flesh of his mother holding him was now dead, and he saith,

"My mother has been reborn in me, and in me remains. Though her life in flesh is no more, the victory is Queen Omega's, for the everlastingness of her soul is what she has attained."

Krstjah then smiled innocently, once again seeming to be only a gentle newborn, and those gathered marveled at this miracle. As King

RAS HERU KING

Khufu Rastari tried to wake his daughter, and his queen took hold of Krstjah, those gathered knew this life would be mythical.

Exodus

Axé!
All praises and honor due to the Almighty, to the I in I,
and to the light of this world, Lord Krstjah Sa Ra Rastari,
Son of the sun, hero and savior, emperor and mighty king,
Ever living in our hearts and on Sirius, forever let thy name ring.
Forever protect the righteous and those that know and love thee
Forever let our path towards Herudom be free.
Selah!

After Queen Omega was mummified according to Rastari custom, King Khufu broadcast her funeral so that Kismet, too, could mourn. Soon after, global royalty and famous Spiritists attended Krstjah's baptism and christening, held seven days after he was born. 'Twas then that the world fell in love with my lord Krstjah, and his supernatural beauty, midnight skin, and sunshine locks and eyes. All this Emperor Iset saw not, for he was terrified of a child his magic could not kill, and horrified to see Krstjah's notoriety rise.

Krstjah was christened Prince Krstjah Sa Ra Rastari, and was ordained for the Rastari priesthood, as he was customary for firstborn sons. King Khufu ended the ceremony by announcing to the watching world that Queen Omega's killer had nowhere to hide under the Sun.

Sweet baby Krstjah was a neonate until the night of his christening, and by the next sunrise he had grown into a bright-eyed toddler. The first three moons of his life were spent playing and singing and dancing around the Rastari castle, and gobbling sugarless cobbler. Toddler Krstjah loved to spin and twirl around on his baby legs, and his smile would infamously remain after every hard fall. He was beloved by his twin cousins and the other children in the castle because he would eagerly play with them each time they called.

When not with the youth, young Krstjah was with the elders, for listening and meditating and reasoning brought Krstjah relish. Young Krstjah loved to dress up in dazzling garments, and thus he was known as 'brighter than the youngest and yet deeper than the eldest.'

Krstjah loved hiding and then inviting castle-dwellers to come and find him by the sound of his golden flute, which never left his side. At night Krstjah was nursed to sleep with childhood stories of Queen Omega from his aunt Princess Hathor, who sat at his bedside. His grandmother, Queen Nyabinghi Tuya, dazzled young Krstjah with stories of the history of glorious Nubitopia, and its kings of lore. And the head of the Rastari Orthodox Church, Magi Chiron Imhotep, revealed the secrets of the *Magical Order of the Rastari*, the *MOOR*.

Every day of young Krstjah's life is a story filled with glee and adventure and wisdom and eidolon heroism, all chronicled by Nubitopian scribes. Yet whilst Krstjah enjoyed his childhood, Iset was busy crafting the scheme which would mean the near extinction of the Rastari tribe.

In his castle in Romilon, in his red private war room, filled with monitors and phones and computers, Iset was feeling blasphemous. Never before had the dark magic of the Ark of Tessarasa failed him, yet Iset saw Queen Omega fall ill only to rise again like Lazarus. Yet his faith in Tessarasa had always led him to greater heights, so Iset moved his mind on to the task ahead, killing Krstjah, his peril.

Nubitopia was a land of many waters, with many lakes and mighty rivers, so Iset sneered as he envisioned the rites of an evil water burial. Iset would start with his old tactics, sending mercenaries through Nubitopia's loose borders in order to stir unrest and perform terrorism. Iset wanted to ruin Nubitopia, and sent in so many evil Spiritists that the country would only ever recover after an exorcism.

In the castle of Nubitopia, in his study chamber, filled with books and potions and crystals, King Khufu smoked herbs from his chalice.

Khufu prayed for strength and guidance in his quest for vengeance, as he stared out a window to Queen Omega's old palace. With a knock on the door, in came word from Khufu's messenger on the true identity of the false king who poisoned his daughter. The king and his island country had been colonized by Romilon a year ago, and that king had been publicly executed and martyred.

King Khufu thanked the messenger, and returned to his chalice to meditate and divinate on the knowledge he had just received. Suddenly, an image of Iset in his war room flashed into Khufu's mind, and he knew that his daughter's murderer was who he had just perceived.

King Khufu reasoned with Queen Tuya and his advisors for three days, and then decided to tell Kismet at the Global Imperial Court. There, Khufu accused Iset of killing his daughter and of colonizing countries, and asked the member nations gathered there for their support. Few nations dared speak up against Emperor Iset, for they knew it would mean retribution and the ruin of their lives and nation. Khufu left without ovation, realizing that war was impossible, and so he meditated on how to assassinate Iset, and he prayed for patience.

But this all only accelerated Iset's invasion plan, for his old tactic after being rightly accused was to get offensive and demonize his accuser. Iset claimed King Khufu was a crazed dictator that was reviled by Nubitopians, and Iset forced other nations to ally with him in this dirty maneuver.

Unaware of the rumors of war, young Krstjah played innocently around the castle, endlessly watched by Crovin, the raven of Jewhuti. Krstjah's early days in the castle were filled with glee and wonder and education, and Krstjah basked in Nubitopia's beauty. Yet at night, Krstjah's soul was afflicted, for he could no longer hear Queen Omega's voice and guidance in the astral realm of dreams. There, Krstjah instead received intuitive visions he could not decipher, visions of an invasion and war and streams.

One day in the temple, Krstjah shared 3 of his visions with Magi Imhotep, and Imhotep reasoned these visions were important. Imhotep reconvened the group of twenty-one Spiritists who were present at Krstjah's birth to give their opinion, after King Khufu's endorsement.

The Council of Twenty-Two Saints was held the day of the second full moon of Krstjah's life, and even St. Tutmoshai was in attendance. Tutmoshai was the most venerated Spiritist in Kismet, and as such, he had been retained by Iset once he rose to imperial ascendance.

In a large hall of the temple of the Rastari Orthodox Church, young Krstjah sat in Queen Tuya's lap, surrounded by those ascended masters. They gave their opinions on the dreams of Krstjah, and all interpretations were symbolic, yet St. Tutmoshai saw impending disaster. Knowing the evil ways of Iset, St. Tutmoshai knew that Krstjah and Nubitopia were in danger in general due to Krstjah's provenance. The council ended after each saint first asked of Krstjah one theological question, and they then prayed over Nubitopia for providence.

And in that month, the schemes of Iset manifested in Nubitopia, and unrest and violence unknown to the land quickly grew commonplace. And in that month, Iset's devious plan to infiltrate and destroy and colonize Nubitopia using the waters of the land finally took shape. Iset had special black and scaly submarines manufactured, which could traverse even the shallow waters of Nubitopia. Though the land had fairly good defensive detection equipment, it prided itself in allowing marine life to live freely, so the waters were its anopia.

As vessels that looked like giant black alligators and rhinos entered Nubitopian waters, King Khufu had reasoned to convene a council of kings. He invited all of his remaining allies, for he wanted to propose they join him in assassinating Iset, and he sent the invitation with golden rings.

The *Council of 13 Kings* was the day of the 3rd full moon of Krstjah's life, and I in I, King Sattvastar of Bharata, attended. King Khufu sat at the point of a large triangular table which we twelve kings joined, and the table was filled with a buffet that was splendid. At Khufu's left sat his lifelong friend and ally, King Ahura Mazda Zorastar of Airya, an old warrior with a gray beard and gray locks. At Khufu's right sat King Brahman Heru Biastar of Swenett, a genius with golden locks and a member of the Rastari Orthodox.

I in I sat besides King Biastar, and we were both dressed in our royal and holy garbs, as we were the heads of our Faith and thus *Magi Kings*. After our feast, King Khufu again thanked us for attending and for our support, and then he asked us to look again at our golden rings.

On each of the golden rings Khufu sent was a phrase written in the ancient Nubitopian language in small italicized characters. King Khufu said it read, "The souls of devil-slayers shall be everlasting," and he asked if we dared become immortality's inheritors. Khufu reminisced on the righteous and angelic nature of his daughter, and then said that only a true devil would murder her. We kings all agreed, and then Khufu said that through the Almighty's grace and his meditation, he was certain that Iset was her murderer.

Khufu referenced the stolen identity of the martyred king of the island, and the ascendance of a new king there clearly backed by Romilon. Khufu concluded by noting that the false king assassin was someone extraordinarily wealthy, because for his suitor session he had paid 3 billion.

King Zorastar was still as passionate as ever at the age of 220, and he swore to see Iset's dead body before he left Kismet. Mystical King Biastar, like the other kings, suggested that the rule of law must be followed, and that Iset had not been proven guilty as yet. I in I stood up, then still chubby and juvenile at the age of one hundred, and proposed a path of dialogue, and to personally interview Iset. Our suggested diplomacy vexed Zorastar much more than it did Khufu, for loyal Zorastar was determined to kill Iset from the outset.

Khufu thanked us for our opinions, then he retorted by saying that his vivid vision of Iset had revealed an evil that was manifest. He assured us that no court could ever convict Iset despite a trial, and then said, "But we shall be absolved by being eternally blessed."

The Council of 13 Kings, which would live in infamy in the following decades, was held in the main palace of the massive castle grounds. The gorgeous isle on which the castle stood was in the center of Peace, the island capital state of Nubitopia, where temples and castles were abound. The state of Peace was in the middle of the country, and it sat where the two mighty rivers of the nation met and split the land into four. To the north was the forest region, to the west low planes and high planes in the south, and the east coast mountains ended in ocean floor.

Nubitopia was a majestic country, barely touched by the conventions of concrete and steel and waste that were Romilon's world. Kismet was a world rich beyond measure, effervescent with beauty and natural wonder, and if Kismet be an oyster, Nubitopia was its pearl.

Nubitopia was largely undeveloped, and one could find cities with paved roads and buildings only in the central cities of the central states. Elsewhere, Nubitopians lived in harmony with nature and the land, for it was so fertile and resource rich that its name means 'Gods' Plate.' The country was a gift to its people, filled with gold and diamonds, black watermelons and black ivory coffee, and Nubian truffles. Nubitopians were a spiritual and laid back people of every shade, and they prided themselves for being beyond the hustle and bustle.

The state of Peace was a theme park of a thousand and one temples and castles, with elephants and giraffes and countless waterfalls. Peace was guarded by 144,000 soldiers and officers, and could only be entered through 3 gated bridges and according to secret protocols.

Nubitopia was a land designed in fractals, where every part mirrored the capital isle in Peace and was surrounded by living waters. 'Twas in that jewel country, on that majestic isle where we kings held what was also called 'The Pithing of the Plotters.' For shortly after King Khufu had said his last word to us did the horns of the watchtower men begin to blow, one after another, incessantly. The schemes and submarines of Iset had finally surfaced in Peace and around its capital, and thus began the dark age of Nubitopia's history.

665 of the submarines had made their way to the castle isle, and from them poured legions of tormented and mutated soldiers. A messenger who had stormed in on our council relayed this information to King Khufu, as he smiled with a regal composure.

In but an instant, King Khufu assessed what was happening, what would happen, and what we kings should and must quickly do. Khufu had had his reasons not to publicly challenge Iset, as all who had done so had been murdered, cruelly and swiftly, too. Iset infamously attacked all critics, by first attacking their character with the same accusation he was guilty of, then by attacking their body. Khufu understood that Iset would justify this invasion as a preemptive strike, and after realizing he was doomed, Khufu entered *Samadhi*.

In a trance, Khufu's *mikarbod* rose from his flesh, and he could see we kings in our angelic *Iyrin* form, and the glow of our *True Will*. Khufu then received a vision in a flash of images, in which nearly all of the kings in the room died, Krstjah became an adult, and Iset was killed.

King Khufu rose to his feet, solemn but smiling, and said, "*Benay hā'ĕlōhîm*, give thanks to the Almighty I in I, for she has granted us eternal life. I sympathize with all of your loved ones, and I apologize to you for the end of your earthly existence, but immortality is now your wife.

"Friends, the accuser and adversary is at my gates, and though we shall lose this battle, I was given a vision of our redemption. Krstjah, my love and grandson, shall one day slay that devilish serpent Iset, and then he shall take our souls to an everlasting dimension. The accuser got word of this gathering, and true to his nature, he shall now bring chaos and destruction, and make history again 'his story.' All this he was surely scheming in the vision I was given; nevertheless, the *Fool* cannot escape fate, so to the I in I shall be the glory."

From the windows of that room and high tower, we could see that the eighty-foot high walls of the isle still held, the walls of *carbene*. Only found in Nubitopia, carbene was a metal comprised of an allotrope of carbon that was used in tools, weapons, and machines. The metal was extraordinary in several ways, highly dangerous to craft into usable objects, and prohibited from being exported out of the country. Carbene is as light as a feather, ten times stronger than steel, and it can absorb and transmit photonic energy, so its uses were sundry.

The walls of the capital were thusly indestructible, and thanks to the isle's air defense system, no one in history had ever attacked. We kings knew all this, so we reasoned that King Khufu had the gift of foresight, for he had spoken of the isle's fall as if it was a matter of fact.

King Zorastar lifted his tiger-headed carbene mace, gifted to him by King Khufu long ago, and then he activated it by rotating its core. It began to hum and vibrate, then Zorastar raised it and roared, "To the Almighty be the glory, for the I knew that Iset's death meant war! We shall waste no more time as mortals, friends, for after a glorious end fit for legendary heroes, we shall be reborn and live again!" And so we kings feared not, but reveled in our chance at righteous martyrdom, for we were truly '*For Rastari and the I until the END.*'

Khufu told us of his foresights of forthcoming events, and every detail would come to pass, even when it took a miracle to be true. He told us that only 3 of us kings would live past this battle, and that they should go and protect Krstjah, but he then only selected two.

'Twas King Biastar and I who King Khufu Rastari begged to find and protect his queen and my lord, young Krstjah Rastari. I in I give thanks to the Almighty for having been so thusly elected, yet why I was bestowed such an honor and blessing, I know not why. Khufu thanked us for the years of protection that were to come, and he smiled and promised to be the first to greet us on the other side. Biastar and I left a room of triumphant *Souljahs*, and so we knew that we must fulfill our obligation, lest they curse our souls otherwise.

We found the Queen, Princess Hathor, her twins, and young Krstjah hiding where Khufu said they would be, and Queen Tuya knew all. She would lead us off the isle after she first led us to what appeared to be only an ornate observatory connected to the Great Hall.

King Khufu had said that the forces of Iset would get past the carbene walls, and he finally told us how they would manage this. The soldiers of Romilon waited at the shores of the island, until finally the 666th ship arrived with one of Iset's chief advantages.

Whilst Tesarak Iset lived, he had travelled the world and imprisoned not only kingdoms and nations, but also monsters and beasts. These creatures could become real again if only a majority of sleeping humans in the area all began to see one specific monster in dreams while sleep. On Kismet, all manner of monsters had been witnessed long after the World Flood, beasts like hydras and vampires and krakens. That day, as the observatory transformed into elevator and began to descend, over the carbene walls of Peace, I in I watched the rise of the Ice Dragon.

Called *Ao Guang, the Ice Dragon Queen of the East*, it was a watery beast with the scaly body of a translucent and icy blue dragon. It was able to spew subzero degree liquid and gas, and it could fill its belly six times over, until it looked like a god's icy flying flagon.

Tesarak had imprisoned the beast in a special fire cage in special chains, after first imprisoning Ao Guang's mind with his hypnosis. Emperor Iset could not control his father's pet, but he could unleash Ao Guang on a locale and let her freeze the land in her psychosis.

'Twas bad fate, and not coincidence, that saw the sky darken at dusk just as that monster flew high and disappeared into the sky. Had I known that would be my last glimpse of Nubitopia with living eyes, I would have bid the land a farewell and goodbye.

Ao Guang crashed down into the great river surrounding the island with such force that it was like a third of the stars had fallen down. The monster gargled and swallowed up the great lake, filling her belly with water, until a diadem began to glow around her head like a crown.

Ao Guang unleashed a frozen torrent onto the carbene walls, and crystallizing ice rooted and took hold wherever it was deployed. After freezing a portion of the wall, Ao Guang would smash it to pieces, until the so-called indestructible walls were totally destroyed. The black ships of Iset grew extended wheels, and into the holes they poured, into that magical isle where the wild things roamed. Only a tenth of Nubitopian souljahs were then guarding the capital, and they all soon met death, after Peace became a war-zone.

Yet I was spared such sights, for as we descended beneath the ground of the castle, I had eyes only for my charge and liege, Krstjah. Krstjah was a sight that no image can ever reproduce, and no words can ever illustrate, and to know him was like the inhalation of ganja. I saw the starry night sky in his skin, and the golden gleam of the sun in his eyes, and in his smile I swam in a galaxy of ecstasy. As King Biastar and I escorted the Rastari family into the escape tunnel beneath the isle, I noticed that with Krstjah, all anxiety had left me.

Krstjah's warm smile and graceful silence were sweet music to my soul, and I in I found comfort in my Faith and hope for a true Savior. Fear cannot reside in your soul or mind, neither in your company or community, when Krstjah Sa Ra Rastari is your heart's neighbor.

As Ao Guang unleashed her fury, Khufu and the kings said their last prayers, and then they began to strategize and command. Khufu wanted to ensure that the scientific knowledge of carbene was hidden from Iset even when he controlled the land. Khufu also wanted to secure the escape of the Rastari family to the high plains in the south, where they would be safe to hide. Orders were then made from that high tower by those great, holy kings that paved the way for Krstjah's return, and saved lives.

For hours the kings surveyed the battle from on high, and they watched the quick advance of Iset's soldiers with Ao Guang's aid. When

Khufu learned that we were off the isle, he said, "Though fate arrives by the avenue of karma, by the True Will is destiny made!"

At this, Khufu called for his legendary gold and carbene bow, and when he held it, he laid down his holy Rastari rod for evermore. The warrior kings donned their armor and weapons, and the saint kings their amulets and talismans, until they were ready for war. Khufu and Zorastar led them to the battle, and they courageously battled the forces of Iset outside of the Nubitopian royal castle. The kings revealed their saintly powers like never before that day, and were like Iyrins up against the devilish forces they rassled.

Khufu seemed to aim into the future, for he fired his arrows where enemies would be, and Zorastar's extending mace was made to conquer. But when it seemed they had started to win the battle, Ao Guang screeched and transformed, and became a truly mythical monster.

As Ao Guang screeched, a brilliant blue light shone forth from her body, as it transformed from flesh and blood into frozen water. Ao Guang had become 'Subzero,' as Nubitopians would call her, and she could now travel at supersonic speeds during her slaughter. She no longer needed to gorge water, but could now freeze the moisture in the air, even until she turned an entire valley into an icy tundra. As Subzero zipped around and revealed her true power, the morale of the remaining Rastari forces was, like the castle, soon torn asunder.

Realizing that the end was near, Khufu turned to his oldest friend, King Zorastar, and he begged Zorastar to live to see Iset defeated by Krstjah. When Zorastar refused to leave, Khufu touched him on the head and said "*Ankh Wedja Senub*," and Zorastar saw Iset's death in an *ivista*.

Zorastar then vowed to protect Krstjah with his life, and to join Khufu in *Haurvatat*, the mythical heaven for heroes. Following Khufu's directions, Zorastar soon after landed amongst Krstjah and us on the mainland, as precisely as one of Khufu's arrows.

Amongst the high planes in the south to the border below, we would travel in shadow for a month, until we reached the *Palace of Makeda*. The castle of Nubitopia was soon destroyed, and after Subzero turned much of the land into a frozen wasteland, it met its nadir. After her carnage ended, Subzero could not be resealed, and she made her home in Peace's temple dedicated to the Principal of Time. The soul of King Khufu soon awoke on the spiritual planet of the Sun, a world made of gold, glazed like honey, and bathed in white wine.

Young Krstjah, the Rastari family, and we kings were welcomed in by Nubitopia's neighbor, where we rested in the shadows of great stelae. We kings reasoned that we should hide in that nation's secret high temples, called Kushaxum, where Krstjah could grow pure as a lily.

Queen Nyabinghi held a funeral for Khufu, and dedicated it to everyone who had been slain during the Exodus from Nubitopia. After everyone had paid their respects, the Queen saith, "The Enemy spilled my goat's blood, and now his horns are a cornucopia. King Alpha has given Kismet a googol new gleaming eyes to view the once hidden methods of Kathol Iset, the conniver and accuser. So let us give thanks for what my king has achieved this life, for King Alpha has now made all of us Kismet's true rulers."

We traveled east through the 'roof of Kismet,' the highest region on the continent, where the stars twinkled just above the mountains. The tall narrow natural stone stelae there, lined with curving paths and spotted with cave openings like artificial doors, were countless.

After another month's travel, we finally arrived at the stone stelae complex that is Kushaxum, and we were met at their feet by the female groundsmen. Kushaxum and especially its mountain temples were forbidden to men and even boys, and these armed warriors acted as groundsmen. After King Biastar identified himself, and the Matriarch of Kushaxum up above was informed, we were led on a path that smelled of vanilla. We followed a perilous path for 3 hours, until the mountain seemed too steep to climb, before we finally met the Matriarch waiting in a villa.

Matriarch Rav Abuna was a brownish red, angelic woman wrapped in white linen clothes, and her aura testified to her holiness. After reasoning with Biastar, the Matriarch permitted us in as the first males ever, for she, like many, heeded King Biastar like *Proteus*. From the cave temple entrance above the villa came a rope ladder, and we climbed up the 33 steps with the children on our backs. Inside the temple were beautiful, ancient murals, statues of precious stones, and strange hieroglyphics all lit by candles of beeswax.

During our months in Kushaxum, we would witness enchanted artifacts and objects which came from the Age of the Avatars. All of the priests and devotees of Kushaxum exclusively wore white linen, and just as did the Matriarch, they too shone like stars.

We stayed in those holy caves until Krstjah's first birthday, and in that time Krstjah swiftly matured, ever cheerful yet ever less childish. He spent more and more time meditating and reasoning in linen clothes, and less time playing with his twin cousins and being stylish. Young Krstjah spent much of his time sitting with his legs dangling over the cliff's edge, looking towards Nubitopia, northward. We kings eventually got word that the world presumed us dead, and we knew that it was safer to remain in hiding to protect the Lord.

On the evening of his first birthday, while we held a fire ceremony in celebration, and watched the sunset, Krstjah told us his plan.

> *"King Alpha had a vision of my victory, and so I shall no longer hide from my fate, but instead go find my destiny as a sun of man."*

That night, after the fires had dwindled, and the stars were high in the skies, young Krstjah meditated on the mountaintop under Crovin's watching eyes.

Krstjah then began to transform and grow, into the body of a twenty-two year old. A perfect black body for Krstjah to master and transmute its blood into gold. That fool Emperor Iset would go on searching for a small blackened child, as Krstjah and we 3 kings left the holy mountains and ventured into the wild.

PART 2
The 7 Legends of Krstjah

The Red Sea

Axé!
All praises and honor due to the Almighty, to the I in I,
and to the light of this world, Lord Krstjah Sa Ra Rastari,
Son of the sun, hero and savior, emperor and mighty king,
Ever living in our hearts and on Sirius, forever let thy name ring.
Forever protect the righteous and those that know and love thee
Forever let our path towards Herudom be free.
Selah!

Under the azure sky and the sweet sounds of Lord Krstjah's flute, we sailed from Kushaxum on top of blue waves and a papyrus reed boat. We kings were crossing a mighty river on the east threshold of the continent, a river so saline that Krstjah could step out and float.

In the middle of the river was a forested, volcanic islet, infamous for being uninhabited thanks to enormous prides of rival lionesses. Rumored to have the finest honey on Kismet, and other wonders, but few had ever returned with their sanity from the islet's recesses. King Biastar carefully recounted the islet's lore, but what are warnings to lesser men are invitations to Krstjah and a typical MOOR. After our long year of ascetic restraint, King Zorastar was delighted by Krstjah's adventurous spirit, so we beelined to the islet with a roar.

The islet was smaller than a town, surrounded by turquoise waters and white sand beaches, and filled with a sea of acacia and pine trees. Shortly after we moored, we noticed prowling and vigilant eyes amongst the bushes before the forest, and they were not birds and bees. Biastar advised us as to where we could camp, and we headed there with no fear for our survival, reveling in the beauty of this paradise. We walked for a time, clearly being tailed and trailed by the lionesses, and finally we came upon the most beautiful lake I had ever seen in my life.

We made camp on a field of red poppies which surrounded the lake, and then the lionesses made their presence known. Leaders of the rival prides cautiously made their way to the lake, and we reasoned that the lake was the only place not a warzone.

As young Krstjah gleefully searched the islet for what wonders he might encounter, the kings and I watched the lionesses and their cubs. These were gallant and regal creatures, shining in the setting sun, and the playful cubs curiously investigated other animals and bugs. Krstjah returned with a carafe of acacia honey and a bushel of grapes, and we dined while watching the sweet lions and the sunset. There were lionesses of all ages, from cubs to aged and weathered ones, and so we could see the beginning of life and death's onset.

Biastar swallowed poppy seeds and asked, "Sweet Krstjah, what is the purpose of this material march from birth to senescence? What could the goal be of fearing for one's survival from the start only to swiftly age and die, as if life is a simulation on evanescence?"

As Krstjah took a deep breath to contemplate Biastar's question, the pastel colors of the setting sun were reflected on his beautiful face. Reasoning brought pleasure to Lord Krstjah, for it was then that he was gifted with his mother's voice, her wisdom, and her grace. Krstjah saith,

> *"Selah, all things and events within time exist and unfold in the mind and spirit of the Almighty, in order for the Almighty to relive and recollect All. Physical time and existence are the latest and grossest manifestation in this recollection, and whilst ephemeral, the body is essential to this recall.*

> *Every physical possibility must become a historical actuality, and all that can be consciously thought and reasonably imagined shall eventually be so. Thus the short-lived experiences of the living do too represent the will of the Almighty, and thus life is a blessed honor that the Almighty*

has bestowed.

"Life in the flesh is no nightmare, Friend, but the gift of the present, and the gift to enjoy all possibilities for joy that are available. It is this endless possibility for joy which leads to fear, for one feels the need to overprotect life, as if life is too assailable.

Friend, life for one who lives in Maat, and according to the rules which govern its place in nature, is the exuberance of youth. Living in Maat allows one to overcome the darkness of fear which is ignorance, with a courage bestowed by the daybreak of truth.

The goal for the embodied soul is enlightenment, and this is achieved by living in accordance to Maat to the most high degree. An enlightened soul may then perform miracles, even physical regeneration and reverse aging, if one's destiny decrees.

"The essence of life, as short or long as it may be, is to live life to the fullest, physically and mentally, so that the Almighty remembers living. Live, prosper, and be in Maat without fear, friends, and as you do so, life shall be a magical dream of endless thanksgiving."

Zorastar had eaten a handful of mushrooms, and whilst listening to Krstjah, he watched the only adult lion, who was weak and old. After Krstjah's last words, Zorastar saw the lion begin to reverse in age, until its strength was renewed and its mane black and bold. Zorastar had been a righteous king for more than a hundred years, but his *Path to Enlightenment* had only truly began after Khufu's ivista. Now, Zorastar was a *True Believer*, and when we looked and saw that it was he that was young again, we exclaimed, "Praise Krstjah!"

Zorastar's body had returned to its former glory, reached at age forty-four, and his locks and long beard were again golden and not gray. We understood then that fear for survival, of aging and even death, were foolish, so long as we strive towards perfection and Maat; *Axé*!

Zorastar was overjoyed with his miracle, and he cried and danced to Krstjah's flute and Biastar's drumming until nightfall. After we settled down, the lionesses returned to their dens or went out to hunt, and we began to chant to the sounds of animal calls. Krstjah saith,

"Yes, friends, the enlightened soul in a perfected body is like an island that remains as the river of today becomes the sea of tomorrow."

Krstjah asked us to meditate on these insights for the night and pray for another miracle, and that perhaps explains the events which were to follow.

As the raven of Jewhuti watched, the Red Star, Mars, began to shine bright in the night sky, until its red corona was thrice its size. Soon after, I heard the sound of a mighty crack, like the breaking of the World Tree, and then the islet began to shake before mine eyes.

A torrent of violent and endless wind blow over the islet, and every living creature save we kings and Krstjah ran for shelter. And then, two giant avalanches of water began to flow on either side of the islet, and this made the islet rumble and sway and welter. All night did the mighty streams flow, and we kings watched as the two banks of the river spread ever away from the islet's shores. As the sun began to rise, the banks slipped beyond the horizons, as if they had become lost at sea after becoming unmoored.

For the entire region had been fast-forwarded, and what would have taken millions of years occurred from just dusk to dawn. The continent had been split in two by a great rift, and this rift spread the land and drew forth an ocean with its mighty brawn. This fast-forwarding created a blazing heat which scorched the islet barren, and the region is still one of the hottest until this very day. It made the water red, too, for in the water was Trichodesmium Erythraeum, which turns red at death but usually looks like hay.

The heat of a million years had turned everything, even the bees and lions, into dust and ashes, save Krstjah and we three. The islet became an island called among other things *Bird Mountain*, and the river became known simply as the *Red Sea*.

The Fire Star Crater

In time, we travelled east from Bird Mountain Island, and we reached the red-hot coast of the sea a few moons after Krstjah's second birthday. We moved north up the coast for a year, finding shade in acacia salam trees, feeding on sweet dates, and riding wild and free equidae.

We reached a holy city on Krstjah's third birthday, and we stayed with friends before moving onto a desert with orange sand dunes. One night, a sandstorm rose up around us and blew away many of the supplies we took from the city, leaving us feeling marooned. At sunrise, a mirage on the east horizon began to shimmer, and its glow gave us hope that we would soon again have water and food. We continued east towards the mirage in the desert, chanting and singing songs whilst we fasted and maintained a positive mood.

When we could see the orange, 8 foot walls of a village, we could also see a line of Bedouins and traders waiting at the gates. When finally we reached the end of the line, we dismounted our steeds, ended our fast, and prepared ourselves for the long wait. Krstjah and Zorastar were overjoyed to see life after our days of traveling in the sand, and they imagined what lay beyond those gates. Zorastar saith, "Imagine, brethren, if there were wine there as sweet as acacia honey, or holy meat as savory as palm dates."

And Biastar saith, "My word, brethren, thou must be desirous indeed, for I in I have never once heard thou fantasize before this." We laughed as Biastar asked, "Krstjah, do the desires of the body align with our spiritual purpose or should they be dismissed?"

And Krstjah saith,

"Selah, the body is to be considered nearly equally important to the soul as is the spirit, for the body is the soul's temple. Whilst the spirit is the real energy, and what is essential to the soul, the body is the abode of this spirit, and thus it is also elemental.

As such, the body and its urges are not ignoble, but the miseducated and corrupted mind may misunderstand and misuse its drives. These misunderstandings and misuses of the body's drives often occur in the milieu of temptation, where cultural corruption often lies.

So it is the corrupt temptations of a culture which make the drives of the body self-destructive, until the temple of the soul is buried in quicksand. The desires of the body are to be tools for the soul's development, for they are the greatest motivation when they become directed passion.

The urges of the body are base, yet they are not in and of themselves evil or sinful or depraved, for they correspond to human emotion. All living entities swim in an ocean of awareness at lower and higher levels, and emotions come from one's spectrum in that ocean.

In time, the soul should come to realize that these emotions are the oars which passionately propel the boat of the soul's motivation. For desire and motivation lead to self-confidence, then creativity and action, and the soul becomes more heroic in this formation.

The body and its urges are tools of the Almighty for the cultivation of the enlightened soul through discipline and refinement. Through the Law of Correspondence, base urges can be sublimated for elevated ends, as the fertile body creates a fertile soul when in alignment; Axé."

In time, we entered the gates of the village, and beheld a fertile crescent of lush green fields, jaffa orange trees, rams, and red heifers. This village was a trading post, where travelers from around the world bartered and traded fine goods under a cool and easy zephyr. There were small wells at every corner of the village, and a large, endless well in the center, and these kept the village wet and wild. Along with fine spices, jewels, coffees, cured meats, oils, incenses, and dried fruit, there were countless harems filled with love-childs.

The village was ruled by a small aristocracy, which was headed by a king and queen, and protected by an army of soldiers and samurai. Whilst lasciviousness was invited, the samurai enforced a lethal zero tolerance policy, and it was not long before we saw a man die. We kings were no stranger to the consequences and final end of justice, and so we continued to marvel at the riches of this paradise. We walked past trading tents full of all things enticing, with fantastic smells and sights, but it was the women that began to tantalize.

Several groups of gorgeous women with covered heads proffered their bodies and services to us, and in time one gave Zorastar a kiss. Zorastar laughed and saith, "My lord Krstjah, of those carnal urges that would drive men to *know* every woman of age, what of this?" And Krstjah saith,

> *"Selah; the libido is the life principle itself, always looking to combine and create new versions ad infinitum. This, too, must be transmuted into passion for the soul to use, by sublimating the libido with tantra to avoid becoming verecund."*

The woman who kissed Zorastar held a golden sistrum and was named Eve, and she was a harem boss who worked for the royal couple as well. Eve procured the most exquisite goods which entered the village for the king and queen, which she then took to them to sale.

King Hiram was a timid man only interested in collecting men and weapons for his ever growing army of samurai knights. With we kings, though, Eve saw beautiful goods that would satisfy the lascivious Queen Mara and her infamous carnal appetites.

Eve invited us to feast in the palace, even at the table of the king and queen, and the combination of her beauty and sly words convinced us to go. As the sun set behind our backs, and the west wind blew through our hair, we followed Eve to the royal couple's orange chateau.

The palace was built above an underground aquifer, and the ground floor of the palace was a beautiful water reserve and cistern. Inside the cistern were arches and columns decorated with jewels, and filtration system that phytofiltered the water with water ferns.

The top floor of the palace had 8 rooms, which encircled a lounge room that had a throne at its head and a jacuzzi at its center. Here the king and queen entertained their guests and lovers with feasts and frolicking, and they were partying there when we entered. Carnal desires of every kind were being satisfied in the beautiful, satin room, and elite freaks and concubines were wild in ecstasy. Eve escorted us to a table near the front, where King Hiram and Queen Mara were seated on their thrones and enjoying the revelry. We kings ignored the debaucherous atmosphere, and were delighted with gourmet delicacies we had never before enjoyed. As we dined and grew merry, Eve went up to Queen Mara, and whispered in her ear the final details of her employ.

The King and Queen and elites of the small kingdom had open relationships, and it was common for either partner to have a harem. Queen Mara was infamous for executing lovers over the slightest whims, and this had earned her the name 'Queen Redrum.' From her first look, Queen Mara was transfixed with Krstjah's perfect black body, his golden locks, and his transcendent smile. Queen Mara paid Eve 8 times more than usual, and with her reward, Eve tiptoed back into the village and the wild.

Soon, we were summoned before the king and queen, and we stood before their thrones with our backs to the grand jacuzzi. The queen was surrounded by half-naked lovers, whilst the gloomy king sat guarded by armed men eager to perform their lethal duty.

King Hiram welcomed us to his palace, and entreated us to have fun, and then he asked us our origins and destinations. Biastar would construct identities for us that were appropriate for each area, so Krstjah never had to lie during such interrogations. Though we had no fear of being discovered by Emperor Iset's allies, we reasoned that only *Friends* need know our true identities. After Biastar deftly demonstrated the details of his fiction, King Mara seemed to be convinced we were not enemies.

Queen Mara saith, "Our kingdom is full of beauties, yet never has a more beautiful group of travelers ever entered our gates. To be frank, your seed and rich color would increase the beauty in our harems, and imagine the pleasure which awaits. Stay with us and be our steeds and stallions, and live as those in heaven live, like princes of pleasure in the lap of luxury. And you," she saith while pointing to Krstjah, "would be my sweet ebony, and I would love you with the passion of hell's fury."

Biastar thanked the queen for her words and offer, and then he assured her that we would soon need to get back to our odyssey. Biastar introduced a pilgrimage aspect to his fiction of our identities, and he again offered up his thanks and apologies. Queen Mara's smile did not waver, as she declared that no god or their duties would take honorable men from a life of such pleasure. She insisted that our quest had ended, and that we had found our pot of gold, and that the name of our new, true god was Leisure.

Biastar agreed to stay for a time more, and to consider her offer, and then Queen Mara addressed Krstjah and redeclared her love. She extolled Krstjah's beauty, and then offered him all of her riches and homes, and then she called my lord the 'Black Dove.' Krstjah remained silent, whilst Biastar explained that though Krstjah had the body of a young *adonis*, he was still not of age. This news only delighted the queen, and she swore that she would tutor Krstjah in the art of love until he was its greatest sage.

Zorastar reasoned that Biastar's diplomacy no longer seemed appropriate, and he clarified our intentions to remain sovereign. He unwittingly admitted that Krstjah was from a land of many waters, and he said Krstjah was not a dove but a black moorhen.

King Hiram perked up, intuiting his queen's ire was awakening, for he was long witness to the extremes of her vanity and despotism. Queen Mara concealed her temper and insisted on having Krstjah once more, but Zorastar's next words triggered her egotism. She stood up suddenly, and said, "How dare you refuse me in my own home, as if I am not worthy of dirty, wandering pilgrims? Hiram, let your men have their way with these fools, for they have strolled into my den not knowing my pseudonyms!"

Hiram was sadistic, for while he took no pleasure in sex, nothing gave him more pleasure than killing one of Mara's adonises. King Hiram watched Mara for sometime, amused to no end by his devilish wife, before siccing his swords upon us. Hiram's samurai were fully clad in armor, and their shining weapons were razor sharp, glistening, and terrifying to even behold. They charged immediately, as if unleashed dogs, and I in I thought I saw my life flash before me in the gleam of their weapons' gold.

And as soon as they started at us, Zorastar rotated the core of his ram mace, and activated his gift from King Khufu Rastari. The mace had been supercharged with energy from the Red Sea miracle, and it suddenly became as if the pupil of the Sun's eye.

An unending torrent of wind and fury flowed from the mace, along with light so bright that it was as if a white hole and a portal. Zorastar held the mace high above his head, and though it turned the samurai into bones, we kings were as unaffected as immortals.

The firestorm blew away anything it did not dissolve, and even a second seemed as if forever under the power of that light. Zorastar hoped the jacuzzi may quench the mace's wrath, but as soon as he threw it in the jacuzzi, the waters evaporated from sight. The mace of light then dissolved through the basalt base of the jacuzzi and continued to evaporate all the waters below in the palace's cistern. A fog of steam quickly enveloped the palace, and then the area, and soon the entire village, as the mace continued to fall and burn.

As the raven of Jewhuti flew over the palace, Mars, the Red Star, twinkled in the night sky, and the steam rose up to the stars. We were in a cloud of vapor, and felt the earth rumble and quake, and in time we heard a beautiful explosion that sounded of sitars. In time the earth quaked no more, and then the steam cleared, and we realized that we were no longer in a palace nor even a town. We stood in a crater as vast as the village was, and as deep as Bird Mountain was high, as if were on the island's inverse now.

The palace, the village, the rams, and red heifers, all were burnt as if sacrificed, and only salt crystals remained inside of a great maar. Zorastar retrieved his mace, and we left what is now called the *Al Wahba Crater*, which *corresponds* to a 'Mare Erythraeum' on the Red Star.

Sermon on the Mt.

Axé!
All praises and honor due to the Almighty, to the I in I,
and to the light of this world, Lord Krstjah Sa Ra Rastari,
Son of the sun, hero and savior, emperor and mighty king,
Ever living in our hearts and on Sirius, forever let thy name ring.
Forever protect the righteous and those that know and love thee
Forever let our path towards Herudom be free.
Selah!

A fter the Red Star Miracle, we kings reasoned we should leave the area in haste, before the cameras and the eyes of the world got wind. We headed north, and spent time in holy cities beside a sea, before heading east to where a vast mountain range begins.

We traveled through plains and valleys, over lakes and rivers, above and around moorlands, grateful to be out of the harsh desert. The mesmerizing views we witnessed were indescribably heavenly, and our bodies were toughened from the effort we had to exert.

On Krstjah's fourth birthday, we reached the *City of the Sun* in a beautiful valley, and decided to rest and relax there. This was a spiritual and colorful city, with so many wetlands, bridges, houseboats, and monsoons that it was as if there was water everywhere. We kings explored the vibrant and spiritual city, and Krstjah fell in love with the cuisine, the momos, and the coconut milk pera cakes. King Biastar was recognized by the local Nagar Brahmins, and they housed us on *Gold Island*, a tiny island built on a lake.

We toured floating open markets on thin boats, and observed hordes of migratory birds and the brahminy duck in the wetlands. We were mesmerized by gorgeous landscapes nearby in the montane areas, with pristine lakes and clouded moorlands. This city was like a heaven for Krstjah, for the mountains and water reminded him of his Nubitopia, the land of many waters. However, the feeling was bittersweet, for Krstjah knew that his Nubitopia was currently colonized and under Iset's orders.

One day, after we kings returned to Gold Island after a long adventure in the nearby mountains, we were met by a grand assembly. The head of the Nagar Brahmins, Pujari, could see the two glows of Krstjah, and felt that a festival for Krstjah was sacramentary.

Pujari had notified all the spiritual people of the country, who had gathered in the hundreds on the shores of the lake near our islet. For the remainder of our stay, people pilgrimaged to Gold Island, and the only price of attendance was a lotus flower colored violet. The pilgrims performed *puja, salat,* and *sembahyana*, they offered Krstjah *pera* and *prasad*, and they lit a fire that they kept ablaze. Despite the spectacle there on display, it was when the pilgrims could finally see Krstjah, lit by the candles, that their eyes became agaze.

In time, word of our regal and enlightened mores spread to a local princess named Begum Nishandeh Banday. She was the only spiritual person of her siblings, and having heard of our presence, Begum decided to visit Gold Island to pray. On the day that she arrived, Biastar was performing the new songs he had composed on our trips to the surrounding mountains and hills. Begum was shadowed by six disguised bodyguards, and though her yellow dress was astounding, she avoided pomp and frills.

The love for Krstjah and we kings astonished Begum, and she was inspired to rebuild and maintain the regions' temples. She asked for a relic from Krstjah, to keep in the holy places, so Krstjah promised her that we would return one day with a symbol.

That night, Begum stayed with us on Gold Island, and we reasoned and chanted and danced and performed tantra until twilight. She stayed with us for three eves, and she and Biastar fell in love that final night after discussing alchemy under the moonlight. Begum reasoned that, "Alchemy is a systematic quest for salvation and spiritual excellence by realizing and fostering the divine within. The primal blissful state of non-duality achieved by the union of masculine and feminine souls in a state of sanctity is the true end."

Before Begum left, she told Krstjah that he reminded her of a mythical hermit in the mountains that she had once located and met. She said that rumors told that he could not die, and then she told us how to find this hermit, named Himaraja Melchizedek.

After the winter season, we continued our journey east towards the hermit in the mountains, riding atop swift and sturdy yaks. Again we traveled blissfully amongst heavenly hills and peaks shrouded in clouds, and in time we were joined by a small wolf pack. There was a male we named Gabre-El, his two wives Kushana and Shamama, and four children of which two were Gabre-El's. Whilst at first they appeared from behind and followed us, in time they became our guides, leading us when there were no trails.

In those days, those great mountains housed a thousand and one ancient monasteries, all breathtaking and filled with pilgrims. Some of these structures were created in the Age of the Avatars, for there were impossible statues made of gold and gems.In time, we kings reached the largest city in all of the mountains, and we knew that our date with the hermit was fast approaching. Nearby was the mountain Shisha, the '*Abode of the Saint-God above the Grassy Meadows*,' and we obtained some Sherpa coaching.

Led by Gabre-El, we soon headed for Shisha, and we reasoned we were close when we began to see prayer flags in a certain order. The order began red-green-blue, then the correct path had only white flags, and then only yellow as we reached the upper border.

In time, we were slowly ascending the spiralling snowy peaks, and on the day we crested the pinnacle, up rose a mighty wind. When the wind passed, as we witnessed a breathtaking landscape, King Zorastar noticed the body of a man that had been frozen.

Buried in snow, in a cleft of rock that perfectly shielded it, lay the reddish-purple body of a man dressed in green and white prayer flags. The text on the flags was written in gold-leaf, so even in such condition, it was as if he was dressed in royal garbs and not rags. His hair and beard were icicles, and he was sitting in padmasana with the same smile on his face he had the day he ascended. His smile brought us pleasure, for though we might regret not meeting him, he had transitioned on as blissfully as he had intended.

The Sherpas had given us gifts and food to bring to Himaraja, and so I went to place on him a beautifully crafted yak fur coat. But upon touching him, a mighty gust of wind flew into the cleft, and as I was pushed away from him, he inhaled and cleared his throat.

As if the wind carried his soul, his first breath began reanimating his body, and Himaraja continued to revitalize as he chanted, "Raum." The snow began to melt around him, and beneath the steam that rose I heard him playing a damaru drum. Suddenly, Himaraja began to glow, and his body was surrounded by a rainbow aura as bright as a rainbow in a clear sky after rain. After thirty-three 'Raums,' he opened his eyes and greeted us, and then told us he had been watching us from the astral planes.

Himaraja explained that he could detach his soul from his body, and astral project around Kismet and through time, to degrees. He had been astral travelling for years, anxiously watching the spread of Iset's evil, but Krstjah's birth had put him at ease.

We made a fire and puerh tea, and after declining most of the gifts that had been offered to him, Himaraja Melchizedek wept. His heart overflowed with passion, and he said that he was filled with joy and gratitude to be in the presence of we adepts. He told us he was born as Uri El Bey and raised to be a shaman, and he told us of the awakening of his first *idi-* or magic ability. When he started to become famous for his powers, he had to hide away on this mountain to escape the Iset's mounting hostility.

Himaraja could energize and maintain himself by breath, orgone energy, sunlight, and ice algae, and he could generate heat at will. He said that all things exist at a specific vibrating frequency, and he had mastered the control of the vibrations of his own energy field.

Himaraja was then 900 years old, and it seemed he could truly live forever, staying safe while remote viewing Kismet. But he reasoned he could now leave this life, for with Krstjah soon to rule the world, he felt he could go on to heaven with no regret. It was then that Himaraja began to eat and drink the gifts we had brought, and he ate and drank rum until it was all in his gut. At night his aura was golden, and he taught us his occult wisdom as we sat in padmasana inside Biastar's makeshift hut.

Himaraja Melchizedek could heal with energy, levitate, move objects telekinetically, and he could divine the past and some of the future. He taught that the universe we exist in is a field of energy frequencies with memory, like a network of digital computers.

"Meditation aims to harmonize the mind or soul to the frequency of the Ether and Akashic field, and away from the ego's tune. When in such cosmic coherence, the seven glands are restored by the Ether itself, so they shall never become diseased," he crooned. We stayed with Himaraja for days, chanting and singing on high, and watching the sound of our voices travel as far as the horizon. We sang and beat drums and bashed cymbals, while Krstjah played his flute, and Himaraja's enchanting voice reached ravens and bison.

Together, we sang classical songs of 'King's Music' - or Reggae- such as:

> Satta Massagana, The Abyssinians
> Abendigo, The Abyssinians
> Forever Loving Jah, Bob Marley
> Positive Vibration, Bob Marley

Stiff-necked Fools, Bob Marley
Natural Mystic, Bob Marley
Sun is Shining, Bob Marley
Rastaman Live Up, Bob Marley
Ziontrain, Bob Marley
Man in the Hills, Burning Spear
All My Life, Chezidek
Never Give Up, Chronixx
Here Comes Trouble, Chronixx.
Jah Pretty Face, Culture
See Them A Come, Culture
Symbol of Reality, The Gladiators
Guts, The Gladiators
Healing of the Nation, Jacob Miller
Fade Away, Junior Byles
Love Alone, Kabaka Pyramid
Open The Iron Gate, Max Romeo
I Chase the Devil, Max Romeo
Love and Unity, Michael Prophet
Righteous are the Conquerors, M. Prophet
Keep that Fire Lit, Mortimer
Message from the King, Prince Fari
Zionland, Ras Michael
Run, Runkus
Lighter, Tarrus Riley
Kilimanjaro, Twinkle Brothers
Faith Can Move Mountains, Twinkle Brothers
Let Jah in, Twinkle Brothers
The Right Way, Twinkle Brothers
Golden Locks, Yabby You

By our last day with Himaraja, the wolves never left his side, for though his soul was enlightened, his ways were as feral as Gabre El. When we awoke, he told us that after meditation, he had learned that the name of the youngest wolf was Shai Mika-El.

For decades, Himaraja had traveled through the astral realm, and he had seen the twilight of Krstjah's advention over the temporal horizon. He intuitively knew that Krstjah was the new Sun of Man, for Krstjah's aura was a purifying radiation that made all things enliven. Himaraja told us that he had visited the palaces of the Celestial Principals, the Elysian dimensions of which there are 7. He noted that the fullmoon was in the house of Ophiuchus, and then told us that we would see him again in heaven.

That night, we kings and wolves pensively watched as Himaraja Melchizedek built a pyre in the cleft, as the wind stilled in the air. When he had readied himself, he said the following, which we began to say daily as the Magical Order Of Rastari's Lord's Prayer:

Axé!
Most High I,
whom we are in fullness,
holy of holy is thine name.
Thine will unfolds in fractals,
and Selah! forever it remains.
I in I am free of dark karma,
I in I am content and in Maat.
Guide mine soul towards thee, I,
from whence it was begot.
Axé!

Himaraja first gave energy to Zorastar's mace, and then he sat in padmasana as gushing wind flew from his still and dim body. Zorastar lit the fire, and as the flames engulfed Himaraja, there appeared an angel in red, as if *Parvati*. She rode a cow, shone a champagne light the color of Shai Mika-El's fur, and she held a golden ladle and a golden pot. Himaraja's violet soul light rose from the fire and crystallized in the sky besides her, and they walked up a ladder into a glowing white spot.

When we awoke the next day, the fire was still burning, and we remained silent for seven days, with Himaraja's aura around us. On the eighth day, we awoke to find that the aura was now only around our heads, and a rainbow light seemed to crown us. The wolves were nowhere to be found, save young Shai Mika-El, who was sleeping peacefully next to Krstjah's right hand. We had had our adventure in the clouds, and we decided to start our journey back down before the day came to an end.

That night, as we reasoned under the stars, Biastar saith, "Melchizedek had a mountain of faith, and his soul was attuned to the Almighty. Krstjah, what was it about Himaraja Melchizedek that truly made him so rich in spirit, so powerful in flesh, and so glorious in psyche?"

Krstjah saith,

> *"Selah, once the ego aligns with the True Will of the Spirit, it begins on the path towards perfection and immortality. This plane of existence comes fundamentally in sevenfold fractals, as does the soul, and the ego is the soul's identity or personality.*
>
> *See the seven colors of the rainbow, and hear the seven steps of the octave, and look up at the seven stars of Ursa Major, the Wolf. The seven immutable principles, the seven glands that are chakras, and the seven light-bodies that have us under-hoof.*

The soul is made of the I in I, the Kama, the EMF, the mind trinity, the body's shadow, the mikarbod, and the I of I or ego makes seven. We are also made of the atoms of our flesh, and the essence of our spirits, and it is these aspects which strive to be godlike in a heaven.

The flesh and body follow the eros instinct, striving to command and connect and copulate, and to be as everlasting as the Sun. The I in I of the soul follows the god instinct, and it, too, strives for immortality, and to be reconnected with itself, the Almighty One.

So when the ego or I of I of the soul aligns with the True Will of the Spirit and the I in I, the soul tends towards immortality. There are seven frequency ranges in which souls can vibrate, and they appear like the colors ROYGBIV in visible planes of reality.

At first breath, the soul manifests in the color range of its former life, and it may grow redder or more violet from the soul's actions and ways. Himaraja long walked up the right way, and used the channel flow of faith and determination to become the most violet in these days."

At twilight, the raven of Jewhuti crowed in the thin air, and we kings awoke to see Krstjah still reasoning on the example of Uri El. Then he saith,

"Yes, violet souls can travel with their astral bodies through astral-time, and some can see past their physical death as well."

And suddenly, I was blinded by a brilliant rainbow light, and when it began to fade, it ascended above us, taking our rainbow crowns. The rainbow light flew off towards the east, clearing a path through clouds, until it was over a peak on the horizon and fell down. Where it fell, the mountain begin to rise, and soon I could see, I know not how, an old man on one of the edges with locks as white as snow. It was Emperor Selassie Rastari, a descendant of Krstjah's from two thousand years in the future, who was also to be a legendary hero.

Selassie sat meditating shirtless, and the snow around him grew ever thicker with every new inch of the growing mountain. Suddenly, Selassie's head drooped in death, and then from the sky above him came a downpour of light, as if from a fountain. Up went Selassie's violet soul light from his body as the shower of light converged and poured into Selassie's cryonic flesh. As the light filled Selassie's body, its vigor and youth and vitality seemed to be completely renewed and refreshed.

Suddenly, Selassie's dark brown body grew as black as Krstjah's, his locks as golden, and his skin as smooth and fine as my lord's. As the clouds rolled back in front to obscure our view, and that mountain grew no more, I heard in the distance Krstjah's thunderous birth roar.

We kings had been given an ivista of the future, and we had seen the day Krstjah was again a world actor and player. The mountain from the vision maintained its new height afterwards, and became the world's tallest, and was renamed the Himalayas.

I in I was so inspired by our journey that I took off my warm clothes, and made a robe of yellow prayer flags just like Uri El's. This I would wear until the day my soul left my body, and at night when I needed warmth, I was joined in bed by Shai Mika-El.

We left Shisha and went back to the home of Begum, and we gave her a dreadlock of Uri El's ancient but still pitch black hair. Begum was overjoyed by our talisman of faith, and she returned to the City of the Sun and Gold Island and built a temple still there.

Yes, these things and more we hermits did see, in the mountains which we did surmount, and twas this we kings heard that night in my lord's Sermon on the Mount.

Heralds of Rasayana

Axé!
All praises and honor due to the Almighty, to the I in I,
and to the light of this world, Lord Krstjah Sa Ra Rastari,
Son of the sun, hero and savior, emperor and mighty king,
Ever living in our hearts and on Sirius, forever let thy name ring.
Forever protect the righteous and those that know and love thee
Forever let our path towards Herudom be free.
Selah!

Princess Begum told us the story of her friend, Queen Devi Berber, who was a member of the empire that ruled all of the mountain region. Queen Devi's wicked brother had imprisoned his twin and stolen his land, and Begum wondered if we could chastise the heathen.

We traveled east once more, towards Queen Devi's wooden castle in the mountains, through avalanches of rain and even a monsoon. Begum had sent word to Devi that we were coming to visit, and she gave us the code name 'the Three Magi and the Sun's Boon'. Begum could not have been more prophetic, for we arrived on the first sunny day in weeks, on Krstjah's fifth birthday. Devi was a world famous dancing Spiritist, and during her performance for Krstjah, she wore a costume of dots of yellow and cyan benday.

Queen Devi later told us the story of how her legendary uncle Mirza Berber and his two brothers had raided and conquered the land. They split the mountains in three, and each had four children, and now the empire was 12 kingdoms, from Srinagar to Nagarland.

Besides Devi, the west was ruled by Devi's vain, pop star of a twin sister, Diva, and her brother's Divo and Deva Manu Isvin, also twins. While Divo was an egotistical celebrity who pledged allegiance to

Emperor Iset, Deva was a man who had never committed a sin. Growing up, Deva was a student of philosophy and religion, and whilst the other children played, he would often be alone reading. Prince Divo was allowed to spoil himself rotten, and infamously demanded to be the star of every childhood proceeding.

Akh Berber, their father, knew that Deva was better suited to lead, but it was Divo who seemed to fit the role of prince and family heir. So, on his deathbed, Akh gave Divo all the land north of the mountains, infamously full of beasts and monsters, called Dragon's Lair. To Deva, Akh gave a region surrounding a mythical river, a land full of swans and rabbits, of alabaster and precious stones called mani. Though his land was much larger and full of resources, Divo resentfully believed that his father had given Deva a land of milk and honey.

After Divo pledged allegiance to Iset, and told Iset of the mani in Deva's land, Iset easily convinced Divo to steal it. Iset knew how to easily manipulate idiots and degenerates, so he spoke to Divo's ego and emotions to ensure Divo would feel it. Divo had also become somewhat of a master in the art of manipulation, and he knew Iset was the world's principal gold-digger. And before Iset that day, what was just a childhood prank long ago between the twin brothers became a tragedy's mysterious trigger.

When the children were young, Divo often became the victim of pranks, for he was as obnoxious as he was economically blessed. It is often said that it is because so many servants wanted to avoid young Divo that an architect invented the *crow's nest*. The very first prank on Divo was played by Deva and Devi's friend Paravati, and it involved an alchemical white powder called kemi. Akh Berber had begun to import tons of the powder in from *Kemet*, as the powder's incredible properties were plenty.

While Divo was off pompously dictating his every wish and whim, Akh Berber showed the kids a magic trick with the powder. Aka added a spoonful of the kemi to liquid mercury, and the children watched in amazement as it turned into solid gold in half an hour.

Paravati soon devised a prank for Divo, and she convinced Devi to take the lead on the prank, and to go find Divo in advance. Devi found Divo in a garden, and told him that they could turn anything into gold, even water, with powder and a dance. As Divo observed, Devi poured the mercury they claimed was water from an amphora into Deva's hands, filled with the kemi. Paravati then performed a dance she had long rehearsed, an ancient dance performed by virgins before they begin wearing a bindi.

In no time, Deva held in his hand a gold sphere, which he was forced to walk over and hand to Divo, since Divo refused to leave his shade. Deva was a shy boy who could not tell a lie, but he managed to play along by imagining one of Divo's tirades. Divo trusted Deva's uprightness, so when Deva gave him the dot of gold, Divo was utterly fooled, and baffled by the young 'alchemists.' Divo demanded their secret, thus initiating the final act of the prank, designed to prove Divo a dimwit by Paravati, the temptress.

From another amphora, Paravati splashed golden liquid, colored by yellow *kumkum*, onto the maidservant who had been fanning Divo. The young servant was in on the prank, and she pretended to become a golden statue, and in so fooling Divo, she became the hired help's hero. Divo would forever believe Deva and Paravati held a secret, and this became the first of many giggles and jokes behind Divo's back. Paravati went so far as to start placing a gold bindhi over her third eye, uncustomary for a virgin, as a sign of the prankster's pact.

And so, on his grand day before the emperor of greed, Divo promised that he could deliver the secret to transmuting metals into gold. Iset was not convinced, but he welcomed Divo into his fold, and saw in Divo a burgeoning new villain in his very own mold. Iset then concocted an especially devilish plan, and supplied Divo with special forces, an army of eunuchs, and a dark brew he called 'iksir.' He ordered Divo to return to him a conqueror of a new land, with a mountain of jewels and mani, and the legendary alchemists' elixir.

In time, Deva invited all of his siblings to his spectacular Centennial celebration, a weekend filled with royal festivities. Divo arrived with Romilon's most famous celebrities, and dozens of ominous soldiers, which Divo called 'security' to hide his hostilities. On the eve before King Deva's Joyous Entry, whilst out on a hunting trip with the men, Divo mixed Deva's drink with the iksir brew. Deva had become a wise and discerning man, but he was intoxicated with joy, so he never suspected the bitter roux.

As Deva slept that night, the iksir spread from his gut, to his heart, and finally to his brain, where it would remain for twenty-four hours. During that time, Deva would lose all consciousness and control over his body, and he became Divo's puppet thanks to the iksir's powers.

The next day, King Deva was paraded into town by Divo and his accomplices during an ancient and annual birthday ceremony. A carnival parade and procession leads the king through town to the palace, as he greets the people on a beautifully bedazzled pony. He then makes a speech on the balcony of the royal chateau, which commences the final evening of partying and the ceremony's end. However, Deva had Divo make a fool of himself by riding through town on not a pony but a jackass, as he shouted gibberish to no end. At the balcony, Deva was made to say deplorable words, words designed to devastate the righteous character and name he had long made. Divo acted appalled, and pretended to end Deva's tirade with a loving hug, and as Deva was escorted off, Divo concluded the charade.

Divo announced to Deva's people that his brother could not control his liquor, and that Deva would be well after much needed rest. Divo proclaimed that he would remain in the kingdom to watch over his brother and the kingdom, to be his brother's aid and armrest. He then quickly leaked footage of his brother's behavior to Romilon news outlets, who lambasted Deva's outrageous episode. As Deva recovered, Divo instigated doubts of his brother's ability to lead in Deva's high officials, until their loyalty began to corrode.

Despite Queen Nur Jahan's protestations, Divo was given emergency command of the kingdom, as he had envisioned. When Deva was soon well again, and demanded answers, Divo claimed that Deva tried to kill him, and Deva was imprisoned. Queen Devi returned to the kingdom, and demanded that Deva be freed, but Divo even threatened her and her army-less land. Vain Queen Diva was of no use, and the rest of the empire remained neutral, so Deva was left in his brother's villainous hands.

In time, Divo began requesting the formula and ritual for making gold, and Deva soon realized his twin never planned to release him. Deva decided to maintain the ruse, as though he did in fact have an alchemical secret, reasoning that his chances of survival would increase then. Deva was secretly aided by ex-officials and concubines and servants, who helped him publish his side of the story to his people and Kismet. When risqué details about Divo began to be spread, Deva's mouth was stitched shut, so that he could no longer speak in a dozen dialects.

As we kings sat listening to her tragic tale, Queen Devi fell into tears, and she leaned on King Zorastar's shoulder. The two of them had begun courting during our time in her palace, and I could see that her tears were making Zorastar smolder. Devi told us that this had all happened forty-four long years ago, and that Deva had managed to live on despite his state and condition. Zorastar gave Devi his word that we would free Deva by any means, and he jokingly named us the 'Hired *Negus* Interceding Coalition.'

Begum had told Devi of our courageous adventure to see Himaraja Melchizedek, so Devi had faith in us and began to rejoice. She held a Thanksgiving that eve for us, and as she danced, musicians accented each move with the sistrum and veena's alluring noise.

We kings soon headed for Deva's kingdom, and travelled winding paths for six days until we reached the legendary Vagus river. When I recall the breathtaking, panoramic beauty we saw while traveling along those green mountains, it makes my soul joyously shiver. In time, we rounded a curve on a mountain, and we finally beheld a small kingdom just beyond a sea of trees and monsoon waters. We rested there on the edge that night, contemplating the story of the twins once more, before we entered the kingdom's borders.

At our campfire, King Biastar saith, "Though Queen Devi's heart was heavy from the grief, it was clear that her soul was light and in bliss. Sweet Krstjah, what was it about Devi that made her presence so enchanting, and that fills me with joy even when I in I reminisce?"

After listening to his heart, Krstjah saith,

> *"Selah, Queen Devi has the Idi of Healing, and she can heal those in her EMF. The ecomorphic field is the metaphysical sphere of energy surrounding your soul and heart, where your emotions are enmeshed.*
>
> *The EMF is the soul's atmosphere and environment, and where Idis of the Heart, such as Intuition and Stamina, manifest. One may get a vibe from a person or place, and this is thanks to the intelligence of the EMF emanating from the chest.*
>
> *The EMF is a star 16.18 meters in diameter when you are born, and it grows a hundred times larger after the Baptism of the Heart. Queen Devi has been baptized by love and understanding, and her EMF is as inspiring as any of the stars on the chart."*

We reached the kingdom before sunset the next day, and it had been divided in two by both the river and by Divo's divisive schemes. Divo instigated a culture of racism by inventing 12 ethnicities, and relocating six ethnicities to the west bank of the stream. The wealthiest lived by the river, with the royal castle on the East Bank, and the people grew poorer as one moved away from the river. Alcohol was made much cheaper than clean water in the West Bank, so that the darker people would pollute their minds and livers.

Nevertheless, the kingdom retained its natural beauty, and the people retained their spirit thanks to the *orgone* energy emanating from the land. Temples of several faiths riddled the kingdom, swans littered the river, and rabbit meat was plentiful and always in demand.

We kings arrived from the east to the West Bank, and the air was tense with fear, distrust, criminality, and miscommunication. The infrastructure was deteriorating, the policing was extremely corrupt, and random, unpunished violence was a daily occasion. The economy had degenerated into bartering and family businesses, and a few corporate franchises managed from the East Bank.

There was enough alienation and self-hate in the West Bank that, even amongst themselves there, there were still more ranks. There, the darkest 'ethnicities' seemed most affected by alcoholism, as we saw many of them loitering in drinking groups in the towns. As we passed through, the west bankers stared at us as if we were exotic animals or royalty, and some even began to follow us around.

Those drawn to us from afar had unique motives, no doubt, yet they all left with the same feeling, thanks to Krstjah's energy. For Krstjah's EMF was a lake of purification and vivification, and its power to raise one's frequency rate is unrivaled and plenary.

Some of those who came near us thought we were rich, and they tried to beg or con us, whilst others thought we were stars, and tried to befriend us. And some of the devout there under Krstjah's EMF began to intuit our mission, and their help they tried to lend us. All those who approached we kings and my lord Krstjah left with thanksgiving in their hearts, and praise for Krstjah on their tongues. They were filled with as much of Krstjah's energy as their own EMFs could handle, until their hearts beat in their chests like damaru drums.

In time, there was amongst the crowd two red sisters, named Apolla and Hermesa Al-Razi, and they were dressed in tights and tutus. They were heading home, and were dance students in the kingdoms' most prestigious performance arts university, called Voodoos. They gathered their courage and came up to us, and after being enamored by Krstjah's aura and presence, they announced that they knew we were kings. Soon, Hermesa said of my lord, "Krstjah is an angel quieter than silence,"to which Apolla replied, "But he is a king louder than dreams."

We told them we were heading for the East Bank and castle, and they said they went to school there and knew the best pathway. They offered us beds in their home for the night and prayed we stay, and they promised to lead us to the east on the first weekday.

We reached the exquisite treehouse of the Al-Razi sisters at the top of a hill, only after ascending the stairs of a deodar cedar tree. They lived with their father, Zeus Al-Razi, a gigantic black man who was the town alchemist and druid, and who greeted us with glee. Zeus was a big-hearted man, who could feel Krstjah coming from a mile away, and had made us tea and fresh coconut milk. As we sat by a warm fire, we were surrounded by distilling vessels, flasks of colorful liquid, jars of herbs, and a decor draped in silk.

We learned of Zeus' wife, fair Leda, who had returned to the east bank without her young daughters in search of a life of vanity. All these years later, he still hoped she would return someday, and he prayed that we would find her in the east before ending his rhapsody.

On the next weekday, we kings and the sisters headed to the capital city of the West Bank, home to the boats and bridges to the east. While we traveled there by public transport, Apolla and Hermesa told us more about Divo and Deva Berber, and the twin king tragedy.

After the golden prank, Prince Divo continued to be mocked, but this practice grew too dangerous when he became heir apparent.

Despite his ego, he had his father's blood, so Divo was blessed with physical prowess, and proved himself as brave as a knight-errant. Princess Paravati grew up beautifully near the siblings, and all began to assume that she and Divo would become the royal couple. But on the night of their Matriculation Ball, when they were all sweet and seventeen, their future as a pair ran into trouble.

On that night, after Divo and Paravati were voted Promenade king and queen by their royal peers at the Ball, the two met in secret. The virgins then found that normal arousal did not stiffen or grow Divo's overgrown member, but decreased it. After Divo left in shame, Paravati put back on her gown, and wandered up the winding stairs of the chateau's south facing turret.

This was Devi and Paravati's happy place, and that night she found Deva there, still in his recherché suit and in high spirits. Modest Deva was in rare form after the ball, and after jokes and an intimate dance with Paravati, the two of them had relations. Deva fell in love with Paravati, but she was not ready to settle, and traveled the world with Devi learning the dances of every nation.

In time, after Prince Deva had become a king of his own land, Paravati returned as a world renowned Spiritist and tantric performer. Deva was married to Queen Nur Jahan, who extended Paravati an olive branch and made her chief consort in the king's *zenana*.

Paravati was appointed the director of Tantric Dance at Voodoos, and it was there that the Al-Razi sisters learned the story's risque details. After Divo took control of the land, he came on to Paravati inappropriately, not knowing that she was secretly inciting Deva's people to rebel. When finally Divo found out about her provocations, he threatened her with prison or expulsion, so Paravati agreed to join Divo's harem. Paravati continued to secretly aid Deva, and because she knew Divo's secret, she knew that as a consort she had no reason to fear him.

Paravati began secretly visiting Deva at his cell, down in the dungeon of his own castle, and she promised the twins would one day switch. She began leaking Deva's galvanizing messages to his people, and when Divo had finally had enough is when he had Deva's mouth stitched.

After many years, Iset grew impatient with Divo's claims of the golden formula, so Iset withdrew his aid and increased taxes. Divo then implemented new ways to torture Deva, and watching Deva hang from a bridge by his ankle during sunset became his favorite tactic. Paravati begged Deva to tell Divo that there was no golden formula or dance, but Deva had decided to take the ruse to the grave. When Divo's eunuchs started throwing rocks at the hanging Deva, Paravati began dancing the alleged golden dance to distract the knaves.

I in I was horrified by what I had heard, and I asked the sisters how Deva could have survived after forty-four years of such imprisonment. The sisters explained that Deva was not only aided in secret by Paravati, but also by Saravati, who was the last golden prank participant.

After Saravati had pretended to be a golden statute, Paravati managed to convince the king to make Saravati Deva's secret *urdubegis*. Saravati thus became Deva's valet, chef, stylist, and his hidden bodyguard, and she remained in this role until Deva became Negus. She had become Deva's personal chef by the time of Divo's takeover, and then became a castle cook to continue serving her Deva. After finding lost stores of the kemi along with a recipe for an elixir of life, Saravati vowed to keep Deva alive until he won the endeavor.

Saravati recreated the elixir, called *soma*, and Paravati diligently fed it to Deva while disguised as a prison doctor named Vaidya Heteru. Deva also continued his pranayama practice, for he had famously taught 101 breathing techniques to his retinue. So Deva had not only survived, but thrived over the years, thanks to Paravati's heroic love, his golden diet, and his mastery of yoga. The name there for the metaphysical force that could be accumulated and stored was mana, and the sisters said Deva's mana was over-quota.

So it was Deva *the hanged man*, and not Divo, who had aged gracefully, and it was Deva who smiled during the sunset performance routine. And so whilst King Divo grew ever more gray and masochistic, Deva grew ever more colorful and beloved, and ever more serene.

As we entered the capital city of the West Bank, we could see, just over a hill, the bridge on which Deva was hung, as the sun reached its zenith. Biastar saith, "Beloved Krstjah, how is it that the prisoner has grown powerful in his surrender, yet the dictator has grown more anemic?" Krstjah saith,

> *"Selah; there is a door to the heart, which must be opened and crossed in order to begin the Path to Enlightenment. This is the bridge which but few both find and cross, for this threshold is the first death of the ego, and the molting of its entitlement.*
>
> *To experience the joy of deep love and union with another, and to understand the wisdom of charity, this is the Baptism of the Heart. Deva's Idi of Stamina is due to the exponential increase in vibratory frequency of his EMF, as it has become the bigger, second star.*
>
> *Just as higher frequencies are vastly more powerful than lower ones, so the second EMF star can store tenfold the power of the first. Thus positive thoughts are exponentially more powerful than negative ones, and but a few faithful heroes can conquer the earth."*

Shortly after, we finally arrived at the mouth of the bridge, an area overrun with herds of every kind of commuter hastily going to and fro. The Al-Razi sisters were adept in the ways of the crowd, and we maneuvered with them towards the bridge like a fleet of arrows. In no time, the people again began to gravitate towards us and Krstjah's EMF, and they gathered around us in glee and wonder. As we reached the gate to the bridge, the herd had surrounded us, and we could no longer effortlessly pass them due to their numbers.

Suddenly, a dozen bridge authority officers noticed the growing crowd, and they dispersed the crowd and searched for its source. The officers spotted we kings and assumed we were foreigners, and they started to question us, as Divo had left outsiders no recourse. They asked Zorastar and I why we were associating with Biastar and Krstjah's kind, referring to their dark and blackened skin. The officers demanded an exorbitant amount of local money from us, and they threatened to beat us, arrest us, and take us in.

Biastar had some powder from *Kemet* which was designed for just an occasion, and he pulled it from his sleeve like a magic trick. He managed to get the attention of all the officers, and when he blew the dust into their faces, they were hypnotized by it. Biastar used his *Idi of Charm* and the *Hypnotic Verse*, and he charmed the officers into believing that we were long-awaited heralds of a new king. They were convinced, and chaperoned us through the gate of the bridge, and finally we walked over the waters of the ravine.

The royal estate began on the river bank and spread up the mountain to the capital city, near the homes of the most wealthy. We could see hundreds of imported swans, and two giant swans that were ten times the size of normal birds, and just as healthy. The siblings, Fuxi and Nuwa, were the children of the legendary beast Vivaswan, a mammoth swan who infamously ate dragons. The giant swans swam near the bank, near King Divo and his entourage, who were all dressed in white and being fed cheese from a wagon.

Divo had *12* lovers and concubines, and they were all sadomasochist that inflicted pain onto Divo in his pleasure arenas. They surrounded him, playing lyres and harps, ruthlessly petting their pet rabbits, and gossiping incessantly as if a den of hyenas. As they all ate from crystal utensils and silver platters, we could see beautiful

Paravati dancing before them just at the river's edge. Then we walked passed six officers standing in the middle of the bridge, where Deva was hanging from the bridge's ledge.

As we passed him, I in I could feel Deva's EMF, and it reminded me of the warm presence of Zeus Al-Razi in the tree house in the west. This was the presence of one who had surrendered their ego, baptized their heart, and was living in joy and bliss, not fear or stress. The officer chaperoning us had to give his best performance to the king's guards, but he finally managed to get us our audience with the king. When we at last stood before King Divo on the river bank, with Paravati dancing and Deva hanging, the scene was like a waking dream.

Along with Divo's concubines and servants and swans, hundreds of Iset's sinister, imperial eunuch soldiers were also at the river. Divo was told that we were messengers of a new ally to Iset, that we were bearing gifts, and had a golden message to deliver. Whilst Saravati was putting kemi in Deva's food, she had been putting lead in the food of Divo, his entourage, and his soldiers. The symptoms were clear to see on them, as they were all thin, agitated, and irritated, and some incessantly grinded their molars.

Divo saith, "Since you are interrupting my sunset performance, your surprise gifts and message had better be good. Now tell me quickly and be on your way: where are my gifts, who is your king, and what message does he so want understood?"

Biastar saith, "Thank you for having we, the HNIC in your castle, and may I say that this is a splendid kingdom you have inherited! But I could not help but notice that man there hanging from the bridge, and we first want to know what he did to merit this." Divo saith, "That man is an enemy of the state, and he hangs above these waters until he confesses the details of an important formula. Until he reveals the secret to transmuting gold, he shall hang out during sunset so he can search his memory and mental nebula."

And then I in I saith, "But sire, surely there is more, for we were told that the hanging man is your own brother and the former king." This agitated Divo, and he saith, "Yes, my brother and the former king and my enemy, and I would not joke about such a thing. Who exactly are you HNIC, and where are my gifts? Be wise with your next words, for they shall no longer be without repercussion." Zorastar saith, "We came to deliver you a message, but our gift is only for a true king, so our business ends with this discussion."

Divo was dumbfounded with rage and saith, "Are you mad enough to come to my castle and call me anything less than king!? Guards, come string these fools up by their necks next to the one hanging on that bridge, and make sure they swing!"

As the platoon of savage eunuchs started at us, Krstjah saith, "If what you seek is the dance of chrysopoeia, I in I can show the way." Divo quickly halted the soldiers and saith, "So you decide to finally reveal your secret and message, as well as make my lucky day." Krstjah removed his outer robe, then silenced his mind, so that he could feel the vibrations of his EMF, and hear the beat of his heart. Krstjah remembered Devi's dance for him, and he remembered when in his youth he would joyfully and endlessly spin as a lark.

As Krstjah began to dance his *Rasayana*, the sky was a kaleidoscope of luminous and beautiful pastel colors, as the sun neared nadir. Krstjah's swirling and graceful dance was as powerful as the clang of a hanging drum, yet as gentle and graceful as a falling tear.

As he watched Krstjah dance and swirl serenely to the sounds of the lyre, Deva intuited that this was the day that he would be freed. Deva had long since learned to listen to the intuitions of his EMF, and something had begun tell him that he was going to be saved by a 'starseed.' The vibrations and emanations from Krstjah's Rasayana rang loudly in his heart, and Deva gave thanks to the Almighty for his freedom. These vibrations also created powerful sound-waves beneath Krstjah, and awoke a dragon living underground named Shesha

Hydrargyrum.

Shesha was curled *three and a half* times in slumber in its warm hole, but the Rasayana made Shesha rise and find a new resting place. Shesha moved in a frenzy upstream, trying to escape the booming sound, but it quickly found itself trapped in a small and tiny space.

The tiny cave was red in cinnabar, and decorated by green, bioluminescent bacteria, and shimmering jade and emerald crystals. Shesha still felt the intense vibrations of the Rasayana as if explosions, so it began to burn its way out of the cave by blasting out a fiery missile. Its roasted the red wall, until the *zhusha* and cinnabar began to produce hot liquid mercury, which began gushing from the wall as a stream. The zhusha rock that did not turn into mercury soon became glowing hot magma, and it burned through the wall and made a seam. The magma cut through rock and stone, until it poured out from the river bank and into the river, and boiled the water and mercury. Shesha dragon's breath did not relent, and the stream of mercurial magma poured endlessly into the river, like blood streaming from an artery.

As Krstjah gracefully danced, swirling his arms rhythmically and spinning in circles, steam began to rise from the now hot, flowing spring. Whilst we kings were attuned to the emanations of Krstjah's heart, its strength caused the entourage of Divo to begin hallucinating. In their vision, the water began to sparkle and gleam, until it seemed like it was filled with gold-leaf, and finally even the land was gold. Divo's lucky day had come, for he finally met his expectation, and witnessed what he knew to be the secret to wealth and riches untold.

When Krstjah ended his Rasayana, Divo ran to him with tears in his eyes and fell at Krstjah's feet, and he begged for the secret. Krstjah told Divo that only those with baptized hearts could learn, and that he needed to sodden his leaden heart and unsheathe it. Divo understood what he wanted to, and he promised Krstjah to bathe in the river until his heart was pure, or he was no longer king. As the last swan left the water, Divo headed in, and he ordered all of his entourage to bathe so that at least one may learn the golden swing.

As the raven of Jewhuti landed next to Deva on the bridge's ledge, they watched as the soldiers and entourage dashed into the water. They had all become completely anesthetized from the lead and the Rasayana, and they never noticed as the spring grow hotter and hotter. They continued to bathe and baptize themselves after the sun set, as more and more of the castle servants came to the banks to observe. Steam soon obscured all views, and only in the morning did we find that they had all evaporated and faded away, and gotten what they deserved.

It was Zorastar and Paravati who freed Deva from that bridge, not too long after the sun had set and they 'baptized' the two soldiers detaining him. During Paravati and Deva's long-awaited and tender embrace, he was able to telepathically give her due thanks for long sustaining him. Deva would have his mouth unhinged by the next day, and his historic speech went on to catalyze a revolution. Deva would soon be re-enthroned, and with Paravati's help, he heralded the beginning of a racist and sexist era's swift dissolution.

We kings rode with King Deva and the Al-Razi sisters during his *Triumphal Entry*, and we masqueraded as carnival magicians. At his coronation speech that day, Deva thanked Krstjah, and called him *the Black Bindhi of the Shri Yantra,* and *the Alchemical Grounds for Superstition.*

Emperor Iset was displeased by the news that he had lost control over the Land of Mani, but he was horrified by the description of Deva's liberators. The international news reported that Deva was freed by a group of four traveling magi who turned a river into an incinerator. Krstjah's reported features nearly gave Iset a heart attack, and he demanded his spies go and prove the words written were not right. Because all of the newspapers reported that one of the four magicians had skin as black as night, and hair as golden as sunlight.

We kings soon bid that kingdom farewell, for we intuited that Iset would come searching for us, and we wanted to spare innocent lives. The *Manikaran Hot Springs* still exist to this day, into which not even one searching for fool's gold after singing vespers in a crow's nest would dive.

Psalm of Sattvastar

Axé!
All praises and honor due to the Almighty, to the I in I,
and to the light of this world, Lord Krstjah Sa Ra Rastari,
Son of the sun, hero and savior, emperor and mighty king,
Ever living in our hearts and on Sirius, forever let thy name ring.
Forever protect the righteous and those that know and love thee
Forever let our path towards Herudom be free.
Selah!

After the world news coverage of King Deva's coronation, we kings reasoned that Iset would at last discover we were alive and traveling east. We decided to again start traveling towards the north, as if the strength of our idis would also ascend as our latitude increased.

We traveled around snow-capped mountains, through deep river gorges, over large deserts, and under skies bespeckled by stardust. The magical, natural wonders of Kismet are more awe-inspiring than fantasy, and to reminisce on them is to bring wanderlust.

For Krstjah's sixth birthday, we celebrated at the Lake of Seven *Waters*, and he wore a 'gold-man suit' made by the enamored locals. As we sang and danced, and Shai Mika-El howled along, the lake's glimmer and gleams made Krstjah's skin shine as if black opal.

In time, a wall of pine and willow trees rose up on the horizon like a wave, and beyond this wall was a region of forests and hills. We soon saw two lines of pilgrims, traveling from both the east and west, converge on the horizon, and they were all infirm and ill.

We would learn that these pilgrims were headed to a place of magic and healing, a place they lovingly called Jannah. The pilgrims insisted we join them, assuring us that all that ailed us would be cured there through magic, medicine, and moon-mana. We kings decided to sojourn with the sick easterners and westerners, hoping to ensure that the end of their journey was not tragic. Crowds of the pilgrims were again attracted to Krstjah's EMF, so King Biastar started to distract them with tricks of performing magic.

When at last we reached the eerie forest, a thick mist above the trees shrouded the blue sky, and it was as quiet as the still of night. We heard a few hoots of eagle owls, and saw the scurrying of monkeys through willows, but there were never any animals in sight.

Biastar saith, "Lord Krstjah, how does the Baptism of the Heart, the planar star, and the psychic idis relate to our Path to Enlightenment?" Krstjah saith,

> "Selah, the Idis of the Heart are milestones for the soul on its path to its own Idi of the Eye, and the Idi that is preeminent.
>
> The six Idis of the Eye include Improbability, what laymen generally call magic, and the most essential Idi of the Eye is Solvation. This idi transforms the soul from mortal to immortal through translation, allowing the soul, for a time, to forego reincarnation."

On the week of the summer solstice, we reached the end of the foggy forest, and beheld a city of four complexes built around a lake. The lake was on a forested hill, and the four selenite complexes resembled giant ice cubes that were both clear and opaque. Pilgrims were approaching the city through the forests and over the hills, and there were thousands of makeshift homes outside the huge complexes.

Jannah had sprung up out of nowhere, and was filled with the families of the ill who had come for the magic of a witch and her accomplices. The majority of the pilgrims never left, even those who believed they had found their cure, and instead became a part of the growing cult. The symptoms always returned, and after becoming indebted by drug costs, the ill would soon be forced to serve the cult as a result.

As we kings approached Jannah, the crowd of pilgrims we were accompanying sent one named Bethesda to solicit our ministrations. Bethesda solemnly asked if we magi and kings would speak to the Queen Witch on their behalf when we all went for our consultations. King Zorastar comically volunteered to act as their king, as the crowd gathered were all, as he, of pale and fair and tanned skin. They shouted in joy at this, but when we refused all the jewels they had brought as payment, only Bethesda showed even the slightest chagrin.

We soon arrived to the southern complex, which was an enormous structure that held homes, harems, and alehouses. Here lived most of the townspeople who were not truly cult members but were still necessary in the operation of this open air jailhouse. The eastern complex was home to the warehouses of drugs and the lake's healing waters, and the hospitals where surgeries took place. We would learn that every townsperson had lost a relative who had gone to that complex and then vanished without a trace.

The western complex held the dark magic academies and the communication companies, where spells were made and mass distributed. This was also the home of the publishing and spy agents, who ensured that certain truths were always prohibited. The north complex was the closest to the lake and managed it, and it was the home of Jannah's cattle, cult, and Queen Witch. This complex gave out free milk and cheese, had constant chanting, and it was a resort built for tourists and the rich.

The men and women who were employed by the cult wore peculiar hats as identification, and so it was clear who was a tourist. The women wore alewife hats and the men wore Phrygian caps, and in their adherence to the dress code, the townspeople were purist. The cult wore white and light blue tie-dye robes, and the few men allowed were all young, with shaved heads save one lock of hair. They were called the

Houri, their symbol was a limp snake on a crystal cross, and they all acted as if they were walking on air.

The leader of the city was Queen Jondes Lilith, a very pale woman with white hair and a crescent moon crown, and eyes like an owl. Jondes was a mastermind and a wicked alchemist, and she could control a monster called Ketos Vritra which lived in the lake's bowels.

We kings followed the pilgrims to the gates of the northern complex, where hundreds of the sick and their families waited in long lines. Their desperate hope had carried them for hundreds of miles, and they bore with them family jewels which had been cleaned and shined. While we were waiting, we saw pilgrims being denied entrance by the gate toll-men, who had deemed their gifts as insufficient. This news devastated the pilgrims, and they moved aside in tears, too weak and weary to even attempt to fight for admission.

We then understood how pilgrims became stranded and desperate here in Jannah after losing their fortunes at the gates and on treatments. As our crowd moaned and feared they would not gain entrance, they watched Biastar use his hypnotizing Idi of Charm on the tollhouse regents.

After the first gate, we walked under an archway, and looked upon the long exterior facade of the manor of the complex. Our tickets had granted us access to the great east, west, and main lobby, which all specialized in different subjects.

The west wing was the male quarters, and from that lobby the Houri gave away food the Queen had 'blessed,' especially milk products. From the east lobby, the Houri gave pilgrims incenses, candles, crosses, and prescription notes for drugs that would address their crux. These notes the pilgrims would take over to the eastern complex, where they would be prescribed a set of drugs and magic practices. We would later confirm what we could sense intuitively, that all of the food and products given out by the Houri contained pathogens.

The main lobby was enormous and magnificent, and it held hundreds of anxious pilgrims waiting in lines for their Houri consultations. At the head of this lobby was an artificial waterfall, before which sat two enthroned Houri priestesses above the pool of water used for the occasion.

Each pilgrims received a consultation with a group of three Houris once they reached the lobby's pool. A female Houri would approach the pilgrim and hear their complaint, as they served them a drink of the water from an ampoule. She then communicated this to the other female, who then chose a divining chain of either moonstone, blue kyanite, or selene beads. She then threw this chain onto the silver tray which the male held, and he then recited a set of sounds describing what the pilgrim needs.

This verse is what the pilgrims then took to the east lobby for their prescription note, which they then took over to the eastern complex. The cult claimed their magic was the blessed food and water of the lake, their divination powers, and the queen's chemical codex.

After paying an additional toll of jewels, pilgrims could gain access to the giant shallow pool in the middle of the manor. This pool was filled with the 'blessed' waters of the lake, and under the non-stop chanting of Houris, rich pilgrims here became enamored. Soaking under the sun, pilgrims would marvel at the majestic moonstone castle of Queen Lilith, rumored to house 18 fairies. Some of the Houri cows roamed the manor around this pool, and lucky guests were allowed to pet them, and feed them special cherries.

Whilst Bethesda's group waited in line for their consultation with the diviners, Zorastar began smoking the ganja King Deva had gifted us. Our souls' frequencies had lowered significantly during our extended time amongst the ill, and that divine hashish instantly lifted us. The enchanting, thick smell quickly overpowered the Houris' incense, and it spread from wall to wall, and from floor to ceiling. When a group of guards asked us to stop smoking, Zorastar frightened them off and shouted, "Is this not a place of healing!?"

When at last Bethesda's pilgrims began to receive their consultation, we watched as they were given a drink and their prescriptions. One of them asked a Houri to prove his power, and the Houri described a deceased relative with a stunningly accurate description.

An hour after sunset, the sound of bells and chimes began to ring out in every lobby, and this signaled the end of the day's proceedings. Pilgrims began to march off in a herd, as if an army of crabs, and they returned to their hotels and homes to ponder their readings. I, King Sattvastar, was beguiled by the Houri that day, for I believed they were a clan of healers and altruistic heroes. But, just as that egotistical Divo had discovered that day he faded away, I would soon learn that not all that glitters is gold.

As we kings began to consider options for the eve, Bethesda gathered up the most precious jewels his clan would have given us. He rented rooms in a luxurious northern complex inn for we kings, and we accepted this gift, lest his tribe would never have forgiven us. We invited Bethesda along with us, and as we passed through the second gate together, we beheld the pool and the moonstone castle. As we made our way along the lantern lit walkways of the manor, we passed stores selling enchanted items such as phantom tassels.

There were tiny elephants and giraffes, elegant wands with crystal and gemstone tips, and scepters that could hum, sing, and shine. The cult had collected countless mysterious wonders over the decades, as the desperation of the sick had long become their goldmine. For so long had the region's ill and infirm given anything as payment, including dangerous mysteries that had been locked away. It seemed we were no longer in a state of the living dead, for the well-to-do tourists now surrounding us seemed high-spirited and gay.

As we neared our inn, the phrygian capped guard that Zorastar had frightened off earlier made his way through the guard's entrance to the castle. He was intent on speaking with his supervisor, and personally seeing to it that we were punished for causing a ruckus and hassle.

While we stopped off in a store of talismans, where the evil eye trinkets seemed alive and watched you move, Biastar was unimpressed. He saith, "My lord Krstjah, of Solvation, and the other mystical idis that arise on the Path, what practices help them to manifest?" And Krstjah saith,

> "Selah, after the Baptism of the Heart has lit a new compassionate flame, this flame must be developed into a blazing fire. Thine own expression is this fire's fuel, and expressing your light shall exult your soul and elevate thine frequency higher.

> "This flame kindles above the heart, and becomes a fire in the furnace of the throat, and finally a new sun in the head's two glands. Like a lotus budding out of water and opening with the rising sun, one must defeat the night of the past by declaring one's new plan.

> For though diet does color the smoke of one's fire, the strength of this flame depends on the unconscious programming which drives us. Beneath our conscious thoughts, we are directed towards the invisible expectations we have based on what we believe to be righteous.

> Karma, then, is administered every day by the conscience, beneath the awareness of the ego. So it is the reprogramming of the mind with declarations and affirmations and altruism, which truly make the soul fire grow."

As we entered our inn, the vexed guard was let into the dark stone tower of the Queen, where she awaited him in partial shadow. The stone room at the very top of the castle had only a cherry wood table, a codex, a crystal ball, and a telescope aimed at the city below. Jondes Lilith slept during the day, untouched by the sun, and she was in a bad mood after just awakening from a nightmare filled repose. The guard had never seen his queen up close without makeup, and after she leaned into the light, he was too terrified to disclose.

Jondes wore a silver dress and her crescent moon crown, she had skin and hair as white as snow, and she had giant eyes like an owl. When finally the guard gave his account of we kings, Jondes ordered a spy to befriend and investigate us, in case we stayed a while.

After a dreamless night, we kings broke fast in the inn's cafeteria, and ate a platter of exotic fruits and pastries that was exquisite. Zorastar was determined to remain medicated whilst in the city-state, so we smoked ganja as we ate, unconcerned with etiquette. Our cloud of vapor made us easy to find, and soon we were approached by a beautiful woman in a silver dress and a wreath of holly. This was Selene Ifa Sulushash, and though she smiled, she did not seem as sedated as the typical Houris, who were always excessively jolly.

Selene explained that she had been tasked to be our guide whilst we were in Jannah, and so it was her pleasure to be of service to us. Selene was mesmerizing, yet it was her grace and sincerity which made her so endearing that we never suspected her to be a *Judas*.

We kings took up Selene's offer, and spent the day having her escort us around the northern complex, acting as our guide star. Selene explained that we had come at an auspicious time, for the Strawberry Full Moon was nigh, and this was when the lake tides start. As Selene guided us through the lobbies, she was a living embodiment of the Houri's ideology of compassion and serenity.

Selene told us that Jannah was a state of healing, centered around a lake of magical waters and built by Jondes, an unknown identity. The cult followed Jondes due to her great wisdom and power, and her codex of formulas, and eventually Jannah grew into a state. The Houri taught that sickness and health, as well as sadness and happiness, were not random states, but based on how one inebriates.

Selene said that the Houri and pilgrims had total faith in the power of the queen's medicines and liberal alcoholic intoxication. Decades of success had also well proven the power of the queen, as her state and kingdom had been built on nothing but donations. They believed that there are drugs for the day, and drugs specific to the night, and so drugs always came in pairs. Whilst alcohol and blue lily was prescribed for the day, a drink laced with blue lotus flower was intended for journeys through dream lairs.

There were 123 different pairs, making 256 unique prescriptions which a 'blessed' Houri might 'psychically' find. Though Zorastar and Biastar remained ever suspicious of the cult, both Krstjah and I became intrigued by their spellbind.

I asked Selene of the source of the water's healing power, and she credited it to the monstrous serpent, Ketos Vritra, and its presence in the lake. After I insisted, Selene led us to the dead lake nearby, which was guarded by men in silver armor with crystal breastplates who were armed with stakes. The lake was rumored to be a gate to the underworld land of magical minerals, Agartha, and this is why the lake's waters were nourishing. Selene then explained their monthly sacrifice of a virgin to Ketos set to occur again soon when the full moon's light was flourishing.

We kings were outraged, yet Selene assured us that the virgins willingly stepped onto the ledge, as it was an honor for the Houri. I in I thought I then saw shimmering eyes in the depths of the deep lake, yet I dismissed this as only a hallucination due to Selene's story.

My lord Krstjah recalled that Queen Omega's favorite flower was the blue lotus, and he asked Selene to tell more of their flower rituals. Selene told Krstjah he could learn more if he found a Dr Oneiros in the eastern complex, and gave us a silver gate pass with her initials. Whilst he and Zorastar headed there, Biastar headed back to the northern complex, intent on discovering the hidden truths of the cult. I in I remained alone with Selene for the next few hours, and thanks to her genuine compassion, I grew enchanted by her as a result.

We spoke of healing, and of the importance of seeing the total wave, like the cycles of the moon, in order to maintain balance. We agreed that love transformed into effective altruism through measurement, calculation, and execution could remedy any challenge.

My lord then Krstjah and Zorastar found Dr Oneiros working in a laboratory where a pond was growing beautiful blue lilies and lotus flowers. Krstjah told the doctor that Queen Omega loved the blue lotus, and that he wanted to honor her and see her in a dream under its power. Dr Oneiros then admitted that he had once courted Queen Omega long ago, and he agreed to help Krstjah as her commemoration. He gave Krstjah a preparation made from untainted flowers, and said the dream ritual was ancient, unlike Jondes' other creations.

Dr. Oneiros said that the time was auspicious, for a full moon provided the most astral light to illuminate the dreamworld. He also gave Zorastar pure blue lily, but he warned Zorastar that using it with large amounts of ganja could make one's head swirl.

That evening, Jondes had the same nightmare as the night before, in which she had fallen from a psychopomp's boat into a sea of the dead. She again awoke in a foul mood, yet she was quickly pleased by the quick work of her spies, and by what her morning brief said. The spies learned that Krstjah and we kings matched the description of four magi whom Emperor Iset wanted, dead or alive. These magicians had helped defeat Iset's allied forces in the Land of Mani, so Jondes begin to suspect we were a danger to her beehive.

Jondes despised Iset, for he was her biggest threat, yet they tolerated each other as long as she supplied Iset with alchemical weapons. As she gazed at our photos, she decided to first drain our blood and any magical power, then sell Iset our remains in sections.

We decided to stay until after the night of the summer solstice, Queen Omega's birthday, and the night of the full moon ritual. Whilst Krstjah and Zorastar played with the lovely cows of the manor, I in I explored the practices which the Houris called habitual. I was given access to the temples which honored Jondes when they were empty, and I napped in the bed of a Houri member. I chanted with a group of the chanters, I studied with their scholars, and I danced ecstatically with them in the manors' center. I passed out the free food, and when I was forbidden from entering into the kitchen due to my hair, I shaved off my long locks. They were elated by this sacrament, and said in jest that I no longer belonged with my crew of regal wolves, as I was now only a bald fox.

My Lord Krstjah was again reminded of his mother by the cows of the manor, for Queen Omega loved cows just as she loved lotus flowers. Under a cloud of smoke, Krstjah reminisced on the stories Queen Nyabinghi and Princess Hathor told him about Queen Omega's powers. After his sixth birthday, and our night on the lake of Seven Waters, the voice of his mother in Krstjah's heart had grown ever fainter. Krstjah reasoned that her soul's time with him was coming to an end, and he wanted the gift of her presence once more, to thank her.

Whilst reclining on the back of a cow, Krstjah resolved to complete the blue lotus ritual the night before the summer solstice. Zorastar agreed that it was time for Queen Omega's soul to rest in peace, and hoped that completing the ritual would give Krstjah solace.

That night, Selene entered Queen Jondes' crystal and selenite throne room to report what she had learned during her day as our guide. The dark room was lit by enchanted candlewicks, filled with black mirrors, and had an altar table made of cherry wood that was petrified. Selene was one of the 'silver dressed spies'- seductive agents who had proven to have some psychic ability in order to become an elite member. As Jondes listened to Selene's account, she telepathically reviewed Selene's memory of my shaved head, and this made Jondes remember.

Long ago, Prince Altai was a man who would not love her, and with my shaved head, she began to see the likeness of Altai in me. After she commanded Selene to arrange an intimate meeting with me, she wondered what Iset would pay her for only the other three.

The next day, we kings all fasted until sunset with Krstjah, as he prepared to perform the blue lotus flower sacrament that midnight. Whilst I in I was helping the Houris milk the cows, Selene reluctantly approached and informed me of Jondes' invite. She claimed that the Queen had heard about my pious deeds during our stay, and that the Queen wanted to learn our ways. Selene said I might gain powers during my visit, as the virgin males were blessed with their divining idis by sleeping under Jondes' gaze.

I in I agreed to go to the queen only after consulting the other kings, who had all intuited that Jannah was actually a state of smoke and mirrors. Krstjah gave me the red hat of his gold-man suit for protection, as Zorastar called me Jondes' next sweetheart and played the jeerer.

That night, as I was led into the palace's throne room, the enchanted candlewicks there shone a hypnotic cerulean blue. As I waited for Jondes' in the fog from a hundred candles and incenses, I was intoxicated by the spices in the incense brew. Jondes finally appeared from a cloud of smoke, wearing a haunting dress that shone like moonlight, which left a glow that lingered enigmatically. Beneath veiled eyes, she greeted me with obeisances and hospitalities, and after offering, she poured me a cup of blue lily tea.

The golden hat blocked my memories from her telepathy, but she acted unruffled when I refused to take it off, and I called it my lord's amulet. As she bewitched me with lies about compassion and healing, I grew spellbound under her specially formulated contaminants.

As Jondes had planned, I was giddy in her presence in no time, and I was transfixed by her silver and angel aura crystal necklace. I tried to convince her that overcharging the sick and desperate was callous, yet my inebriation had made my arguments feckless. It was only when I wholeheartedly objected to human sacrifice in all circumstances did our conversation grow heated. She laughed off my concerns, so I bid her goodnight, as she repeated that I would understand after the next sacrifice was completed. After I left, Jondes would go on to mistake the warm feelings she had received from my EMF as, instead, love at long last. Inspired by her delusion, she would go on to drink over a dozen love potions and perform *18* love rituals before the night passed.

Beneath the waxing moon's light, and the gaze of Zorastar and the cows, Krstjah fell asleep under a holly tree thanks to the blue lotus. He awoke in a dream in the same space, and only after a mighty gust of wind flew from him towards the moon did he notice. The wind cleared away clouds, revealing not the moon, but a shining Queen Omega, on a throne of clouds and encircled by a ring of light. A silver thread connected Krstjah to Queen Omega, and upon realizing this Krstjah began to grasp onto the thread with all his might.

Queen Omega told Krstjah that she loved him dearly, and that she would now watch down on him as if the moon were her eyes. Krstjah thanked his mother for all of her love, and before she and the thread vanished, she gave him a magical sound to memorize.

Krstjah awoke before sunrise to the sight of an extravagant moonbow, whose iridescence painted the cows prismatically. I too received a rainbow of sorts, after Jondes sent me a japamala made of angel aura crystal, as a way to express her interest emphatically. Though I was dazzled by the japamala, I was embarrassed by a dramatic public display of affection which I had no plans to reciprocate. I was told that this gift meant that I was becoming a new 'Daimon', which was a consort to the queen with the powers of a chief magistrate. I graciously took the talisman, and declared for all to hear that I would personally give all due thanks and gratitudes to the lovely queen. Yet, I knew that I could not ignore the euphoric vibrations which had enraptured me that day I became enamored by Selene.

Zorastar was still in a jesting mood, and said that it was time for me to go 'baptize' the heart of 'the wicked witch of the north.' After a laugh was shared by the group, Zorastar could see I was in no humor for jokes, and he ceased from thenceforth. Biastar smiled, then saith, "Lord Krstjah, what is the next gradation towards Solvation after the baptism and flame of the heart?" Krstjah listened for Queen Omega but heard her not, then saith,

> *"Selah, in time the growing flame will become a blazing fire, and its dance will start. And while expressing its light, the magic of a new dance may give rise to the soul's star, after awakening the Flow of the Heart."*

As the kings began to leave the cafeteria and discuss their activities for the day, I quickly made my way back to my room with a dart. Krstjah's words put my mind at ease for the remainder of the day, for instead of considering Jondes' proposal I wrote a psalm to pray:

The Psalm of Sattvastar

In Krstjah, my lord and guide, do I console,
The waterman in the moon-boat of my soul.
For Krstjah guides I in I in what is essential,
And his love and sincerity are his credentials.
Krstjah bathes I in I in the river of stamina,
And ferries I in I over the waters of nirvana,
I in I hear Krstjah's voice in silent meditation,
Blessing and confirming I in I like affirmations.
Knowledge and understanding comes from thee,
And your words rise up in me like a blue lily.
From mine depths towards mine exalted eye,
Through a throat and from a mouth free of lies.
Thou art the melody in music,
and the muse of poets,

the magic in mantras and the heka in all heroics.
Glorious is thy presence, Krstjah,
hallowed be thy names,
thou art the silver in smoke, and the gold in flames,

As Krstjah and the kings celebrated the solstice and honored Queen Omega's birthday, I in I sat alone in front of our inn's fireplace. As I finally lay down my raven's quill, a robotic white owl flew into the window, and it proceeded to scan the entire space. The owl flew away when it was finished, and then the fire and all the lights dimmed low, as a hidden door in the bookcase opened. The next events catalyzed a range of emotions in me from baffled anxiety all the way to a feeling both titillating and jocund.

For in from the door walked an obscure figure, nearly invisible beneath a cloak of refraction, which unveiled its face to be Selene. She held a special bell in her hand which could inhibit monitoring devices in the area, so long as we spoke in whispers and heard its ring. Selene desperately needed me to know her story, yet she was unnerved into murmuring, so I gave her some of our royal ganja. Selene gathered her courage and trust in me, and then detailed her true identity, and all of the nightmarish realities of Jannah.

Selene was a member of a family that had vowed to watch over Jondes Lilith until the day they witnessed her meet her just desserts. Selene told me that the Houri medicine was primarily snake venom and pain relievers, and it was not riches Jondes wanted, but worse. Jondes Lilith created Jannah to be her flytrap, where she could combine the fluids of victims so that her body could be regrown. For Jondes was cursed with a condition which caused any light stronger than moonlight to burn her skin and flesh down to the bone.

Centuries ago, Jondes was a princess and the military alchemist of a kingdom that was in a hundred year war with its neighbor. As the alchemical weapons expert, Jondes delighted in the grisly and ghastly effects of her formulas, and in the notoriety of her labors. She was the eldest princess and first in line to become queen, but she was ghostly pale and had white hair, and never once a suitor. For many, personality and intelligence could overcome poor looks, yet Jondes' appearance undermined her and her mind of a computer.

One day, a prince of the neighboring kingdom, bold and bald young Prince Altai, arrived by chance to her father's court. His ludicrous peace proposals were so comical, the king was charmed, and he too vowed to settle their differences by any resort.

At Prince Altai's royal reception, preparations were made to ensure he would court Princess Jondes, yet he fell for her sister instead. As peace was on the horizon and all celebrated the young couple's love, Jondes grew green with envy, and she began to see as red as bloodshed. Through callous deception and manipulation, Jondes instigated a new war that began just before the royal couple's first anniversary. Jondes sold increasingly destructive weapons to both nations, intent on ruling over the few who survived as a sorceress and mercenary.

Finally, Jondes gave her father's army a forbidden formula called Quicksilver, with silver flames which endlessly burned and spread until a new moon. Its silver flames did not combust what it engulfed, but surrounded it in a cool breeze, and inhalation of its silver vapor meant one's doom. When finally the moon was new, the stench of rotting flesh could poison birds in flight, and Jondes was exiled by those who survived. Her experiments with Quicksilver had caused strong light to become a radiation to her, so any light stronger than the moon made her run and hide.

In time, Jondes came across the dead lake in a dead forest, and at its banks stood a massive cross made of the enchanted crystal. After she managed to shatter the cross into pieces with her magic, the monster the crystal was imprisoning rose from the lake's abyss. The iridescent and serpentine skin of the beast had the very same design as the crystal, and it had a dragon's face and curved horns. The beast was set to consume her, but a crystal shard she held amplified the toxicity of her EMF, and the beast saw her spiritual thorns.

Jondes then realized she could control the beast Ketos with the crystal, as it gave her a weak telepathic connection to the beast's powers. She used her alchemy and this power to build up the facade of Jannah as a place of life and healing, when the truth was far sourer.

By killing the pilgrims slowly with the beast's venom, and prescribing abortions, Jannah had a constant flow of fluids and hormones. Added with the reproductive floods of virgin Houris, Jondes was able to create flesh when needed, which she grafted onto her bones. The silver knights fed the bodies to the beast, and the Houris took mandatory drugs that keep them docile and jolly. Jondes' bite on their necks filled them with Ketos' blood and brief telepathic powers, and their recital of one of the verses would complete the folly.

Selene then confessed to constantly being in danger, and she began to weep from the many years of anxiety and dread. "Devils hate holly trees," she said, so her family surrounded Jannah with them to trap Jondes, and Selene wore a holly wreath on her head. I in I promised to stop Jondes, and then I doffed her wreath and caressed her tear-soaked and supple cheeks. That night, after I called her Cundi Bhagavati and she called me Guanyin, we knew love, and danced across the inn's silk sheets.

Selene was gone when I awoke, and though the day would prove climatic, I remained throughout it as blissful as a Houri is jolly. I carried around two signs of affections that day, for on my bed-stand that morning, next to my japamala, was Selene's wreath of hollies.

Before breakfast, we kings discussed the true nature of Jannah, and the other kings were not surprised in the least by my revelations. Biastar had discovered the very same horrific truths of poisoning and druggings and disappearances during his investigations. We vowed to confront Jondes that evening and interrupt the full-moon sacrifice ritual before any virgins were fed to the monster.

Zorastar rubbed my bald head and chuckled, and Biastar said that I could now fully absorb the light of the moon with the tonsure. I put on Selene's crown of hollies, and as Zorastar laughed, I told him that I would have the last laugh when Jondes read his memory. Yet this would jeopardize Selene's life, for when Jondes saw me with the wreath, Selene immediately became her primary enemy.

That evening, there was a supermoon, a lunar eclipse, and a moon dog, and nearly two thousand people were at the lake for the sacrifice. We kings stood in between the ledges where the victim was placed and where Jondes gesticulated, ready to stop her at any price.

Jondes arrived in a tall silver conical damask hat made of the angel aura crystal, and she held a dazzling crystal wand for the occasion. After the first victim was led out onto the ledge in inebriated ecstasy, Jondes declared that there would be a special deviation. Jondes announced that tonight, Ketos Vritra would feed on a cherry-less Houri, and that one Houri had just lost her virginity. To my shock, a bound and gagged Selene was brought out, as Jondes smirked directly at me, with a heart filled with acridity.

When finally Selene replaced the virgin on the ledge, Jondes began to murmur and wave the wand around, summoning the beast. Krstjah told us to chant Queen Omega's magical phrase, '*Haum Raum*,' and he told us to visualize that Selene was being released.

As we chanted, Ketos rose up from the water, and as it snarled and shimmered in the moonlight, it was awe-inspiring to behold. Yet time itself began to rapidly slow, and when Ketos was prepared to launch at Selene, it took a minute for a second to unfold. As we kings continued chanting, surrounded by living creatures now suspended in time, steam began to blow from our mouths. It was then that the miracle began, as the final witnesses were in place, and Crovin landed next to onlooking silver-coated monkeys and owls.

Suddenly a feeling of love and bliss spread over me as I closed my eyes, and a kaleidoscope bathed the darkness of my inner eye. And suddenly I saw my mikarbod wearing the gold-man suit and japamala, and I was in a dark cave lit by light the color of the sky. I felt the presence of a giant snake floating in the air around me, and finally I could dimly see the radiant face of Ketos Vritra. The powers of the crystal and the Omega chant had given me the Idi of Telepathy, and I had traveled into the beast's inner cathedral.

I paid my respects and introduced myself, and I asked Ketos why it was allowing Jondes to control and corrupt it, and to damn its soul. I learned its true name, Ahi Leviathan, and Ahi said that after she pricked her EMF on Jondes, the witch's venom had taken hold. I offered to purify away the poison of Jondes' quicksilver aura, only if Ahi agreed that the witch must be stopped at any cost. Ahi agreed, and said it only wanted to fulfill its duty to guard this gate to the underworld, and put an end to Jondes' holocaust.

Before I left that inner space, I expected Jondes' poison in Ahi to disappear, and I gave thanks even before I sensed it had disintegrated. As the normal rhythm of time returned, Ahi continued its lunge, but it changed its direction towards where Jondes was located. Ahi swallowed the witch and the enchanted crystals she wore, so Jondes remains alive until this day in the belly of the beast. She swims amongst the fermented bodies of her victims, and on their unbound fluids will that quicksilver devil of envy forever feast.

After Ahi swallowed Jondes, the pain of consuming the angel aura crystals on her put Ahi into shock, and it began to spin and sway. In a fit of convulsive pain, Ahi spun faster and faster, and as it finally sank into the lake, it created a whirlpool in its dismay. A tempest of wind began, and thunder rang out, as Ahi was shot from the lake high into the sky towards the red supermoon. As it fell back down into the lake, Ahi brought with it clouds and the winds, and when this entered the whirlpool, it created a typhoon.

The typhoon sucked up the buildings of the complexes, the Houris, the cherries and cheese, the drugs and the beer. When complete, the typhoon fell into the lake, and soon a few pilgrims painted silver in mud, and sky colored tree frogs, began to appear.

Suspecting that Jondes had alerted Iset to our presence in Jannah, we kings continued north, as Selene became the leader of the survivors. The lake is still there to this day and still dead, and thanks to its infamy, it has many visitors each year but nearly no divers. It is rumored that many see the glimmer of silver or crystals in the lake, and others hear the devil's whispers while on the lake's banks. The locals now call it Lake Shaitonkol, or Lake of Devils, and we now call Omega's mantra the *Shema Omega*, and give thanks.

Krstjah was delighted by my psalm, and after he called it his gift for his upcoming birthday, he embraced me with joy and love. I in I promised Selene I would return for her after our journey ended, even if I had to travel to her from the stars above.

The Rising Sun

Axé!
All praises and honor due to the Almighty, to the I in I,
and to the light of this world, Lord Krstjah Sa Ra Rastari,
Son of the sun, hero and savior, emperor and mighty king,
Ever living in our hearts and on Sirius, forever let thy name ring.
Forever protect the righteous and those that know and love thee
Forever let our path towards Herudom be free.
Selah!

Soon after we kings left Shaitonkol, the state-of-the-art aircraft of Iset's elite guard arrived and hovered over the lake's waters. The Moonstone Palace mostly remained, and it would wear a billion cracks until the day the palace was restored by the hero of potters. Iset sent all 186,000 of his infamous soldiers, the Immortal Vanguard, who bore silver masks with the face of the Evil One. Iset's scheme was to kill Jondes along with we kings, and then steal all of the enchanted objects donated by the pilgrims of the region.

The item Iset most coveted was Jondes' codex of spells and metaphysical blueprints, which detailed all of her alchemical weapons. Without this codex, Iset could not fully control the magical tools she sold him, nor the monsters like Subzero in his collection.

In addition to enchanted objects, Jondes had also provided Iset with other essential weapons in his arsenal of colonization. Chief amongst these were the poisons Iset used against targets, and the masks of living flesh he used in covert operations. Iset had worn one of Jondes' masks in order to poison Queen Omega, and he had poured the devil's brew from a Jondes' chalice. The forces of Iset searched the area for months looking for that codex, but they could not locate it, not even in the broken palace.

In two years time, Iset had lost control of the both the Land of Mani and the means to control his beasts, and Iset was triggered by loss. Enraged, Iset then sent a seventh of his entire army to the region, determined to kill young Krstjah once and for all, and remain boss.

As we kings traveled north, above our heads flew the black jets and aircrafts of Romilon forces, as if menacing birds of prey. They spread throughout the region, past borders and above all jurisdictions, settling in all nearby countries, to the locals' dismay. We had no fear of being detected by the enemy's eyes in the sky, for Biastar had taught us how to move like smoke in shadows. With Krstjah and Shai in the center, and one of us always to the left, to the right, and before them, we traveled as swift as arrows.

For forty nights, we vigilantly searched the sky for Romilon jets and drones, and we slept inside rock cracks and wrinkles. As I became familiar with the location of every star and constellation, my eyes learned the rhythm of a dozen stars' twinkle. We then arrived at a kingdom of fire and ice called Gidipride, which had suddenly started to become a frozen tundra. Worse, a new heretical king and the vicious enforcement of his new religion had torn Gidipride's national unity asunder.

King Galileo Anero Serapis was the self-proclaimed son of the Naten, the god of solar wind, and Naten became the state god by decrees. As god-king, GAS declared that he was the only priest, and stripped from the priest-politicians of Amen, the old god, all their prestige. GAS taught that there was no god above him and Naten that could judge humans, and one may do as they like if they have the might. Thanks to his deceptive magic tricks and the twisted ethics he promoted, GAS became the Church of Romilon's new living Christ.

Before nearing the southern gates, we kings stopped to shed our priestly robes, as if we were bearded dragon lizards. We placed on the indigo magician costumes we had worn at King Deva's coronation, and disguised ourselves as traveling wizards.

Gidipride was a land of plastic surgery and illusion, where gangs and mobs and families of Natenites or Amenites had local control. The streets of the now icy land were lit by street-lamps and torches, but those had not stopped the citizen's hearts from becoming cold. GAS' self-centered culture and his cultural wars had divided the people, and a cycle of violence had colored hearts in malice. The national pastime of the country had become watching imprisoned Amenites be publicly 'tried by sabertooths' in GAS' Circus Spectacalis.

As we kings walked through an open air marketplace, puffed up and plastic groups of Natenites laughed and behaved like snobs. They were entitled idiots, and theirs was the new culture of 'you-only-live-once' that was supported by their god-king and mobs. Amenites had then for years been subjected to unpunished random violence, unjustified imprisonment, and public executions at the Circus.

So Amenites rarely appeared in public alone, and when they did, their fear, anxiety, and trepidation were visible on the surface. The presence of the Romilon Army and IV emboldened the Natenites even more, yet they would learn the taste of their own medicine. The soldiers of the Empire are the most entitled and unhinged men on Kismet, and they treated the Natenites as but worthless denizens.

Whilst walking along a path beautifully lit with several dazzling torches, we stopped to admire the flames in the still and icy wind. Biastar then asked, "Lord Krstjah, after the dance of the soul's fire ignites the Flow of the Heart, how does the soul's fire next ascend?" Krstjah saith,

> *"Axé, after flow and expression change the candle's fire into a small star, one shall in time arrive at the highest plateau. At this thirty-third level, called the Bedroom of the Bride, a new path emerges, and the candle's starlight grows dark with a*

black-light glow.

In this darkness, as one masters one's Idi of the Heart, and awakens new idis, the Third Eye will finally open from spiritual sensitivity. Then with new eyes and a new awareness to the Holy Spirit, one begins to see through the dark with the light of Synchronicity."

As we continued through this town center, we were overwhelmed with the amount of raw beef that was being sold and consumed. It was for centuries illegal to kill bulls, since they were the symbol of the sky god Amen, but Amenites were now forced to sell their heirlooms.

As we passed a place where unscrupulous Amenites sold stolen meat to eager and willing Natenites, a sales dispute became violent. The Natenite had demanded a lower price, and then took beef without paying, but the Amenite's swift blade left him stiff and silent. As the Natenite breathed his last breath in front of unsympathetic eyes, the Amenite merged into an unsuspecting crowd. In a short time, an oblivious shopper tripped over the body, now swimming in warm, red, raw blood, and she began to scream out loud.

A commotion of onlookers, officers, and soldiers grew larger and larger just as we kings continued on our journey through the town. The lurid glitz of the Natenite culture and advertisement was hypnotizing and nauseating, and we endured it all until sundown.

As we contemplated accommodation for the night, we saw the Amenite murderer from earlier being chased down by Natenites. His frantic escape through the Natenite crowd proved his undoing, for a new crowd formed from those he jostled during his flight. His Natenite pursuers arrived and proceeded to beat and stomp him mercilessly, as the Natenite mob cheered. Zorastar had seen enough, and as we started over to the crowd, a voice behind us called out to us before we could get near.

We turned to find an aged, red-skinned man with long dreadlocks and indigenous clothes, who was selling sinapis oil and charlock. He spoke the same I-language of the ancient Nubitopians, and said, "Idren, do not concern thine self with the snakes in a field of hemlock. There is no justice amongst the heathen there, my brethren, and I in I sense that the I has come to this land so that justice is redeemed." As we turned to look back at the growing mass of giddy onlookers, Romilon soldiers and members of the IV arrived on the scene.

The red man had had a vision, in which he talked with walking flames, and upon seeing the convection lines of our aura, he knew we were the fire. He then saith, "I in I am Agna Agya Agni, and I in I shall be thine guide whilst the I fulfills its good deed in this land of strife and quagmire."

Agna offered to hide us away from soldiers and accommodation for the night, and we followed him to a village along the outskirts. Agna was a part of a group called the Dreads, and they were a community of vegetarians who lived communally and nomadically in yurts. The Dread culture had been native to the land before even Amen worship, and under GAS they remained tolerated but demonized. However, as the new Natenite culture encouraged rebelliousness and non-conformity, by some Natenites the Dreads were now idolized.

The Dreads deified the spirit of nature in all living and organic forms, and the best symbols of this spirit in all things was smoke and fire. The twelve tribes of Dreads all had slightly different symbolic associations, yet all Dreads daily gave offerings to local never-ending pyres. The most extreme Dreads refused all 'unnatural' human customs, harmed not even ants, and had locks down to their soles.

Yet theirs was a people long traumatized by repression, fear, and group guilt, so only the elders, like Agna, could see our flaming souls. Informants and the criminally minded hid amongst their community, so mistrust was now always in the midst of Dread gatherings. So now, the wisest amongst them spoke the truth only in symbols and scatterings, which to the uninitiated sound like jabberings.

The Dreads grew the essential food crops, seeds, and oils that feed not only the nations' cows but also its ever present, fiery lamps. Agna took us to the biggest yurt, in the middle of all others, a place called the House of Pinecones, where the Dread elders were encamped.

After placing some charlock onto the pyre, Agna asked us to sit and wait at dining tables in the yurt as he went to fetch Dread food for us. Homely Dreads of all ages and tribes came to feed the fire and noticed our magic attire, before finally food was set before us. To the delight of my lord Krstjah, Agna had brought us steamy pies sweetened with raw honey and filled with elder and crowberries. Unbeknownst to us, this created whispers and rumors, for the Dreads by religious custom were to eat nothing that day but cranberries.

Agna said that he wanted us to try his favorite food, and be as comfortable amongst his people as would be the King of the Dreads. Whilst we ate, Agna recounted the recent history of Gidipride and its new ice age, of GAS and Naten, of how it all began and still spreads.

Galileo Serapis was a man with long, golden hair, a shimmering beard, blue eyes, and a smile which both women and men adored. He had been just an illegitimate son of the king, and had never imagined he would ascend the throne before his father was no more. His mother was of a priestly caste bred to divinate, and she had snuck into the king's chambers and used love potions to make him breed her. She was hell bent on possessing power denied to her by her coven, and had devised a plan that would make her seed the new leader.

After the prince and heir apparent died mysteriously soon after the king, GAS emerged as a potential candidate amid controversy. Through deception, illusion, and trickery, GAS was crowned king after he seemingly found a lost pyramid and fulfilled an old prophesy.

GAS knew that his father had only begun to worship Naten as a ploy to take back some of the political power of the Amen priest. GAS and his mother took this ploy to its extreme, and claimed that GAS was the avatar of Naten, and the son of the Amen in the East. After his coronation, GAS declared that Naten had become the godhead, and had become more important than even Amen Tengri. Many continued to secretly worship Amen, and the priest of Amen maintained their sway, so GAS finally went to the extremity.

GAS published a supposedly 'revealed text' called 'The Book of Me,' which encouraged self-idolatry, self centeredness, and vice. GAS sanctified any and all debauchery of those who idolized him, and was thusly named the Church of Romilon's Christ. After receiving the endorsement of Iset and the empire, GAS stripped all of the priests of their power and became dictator. Rumors of civil war and alleged assassination attempts soon led to mass imprisonments, and soon Gidipride came to its nadir.

A culture of violent Natenite patriotism led to regular public executions, and soon violent entertainment was the norm. GAS also built a new train system to modernize and connect the country, and as it spread south, so too did an odd and perpetual ice storm. This new ice age landed like an icy comet, and its drastic new conditions quickly uprooted centuries of horse and bull farming. But it was the degree to which hate and fear had taken over the people of Gidipride which Agna found most alarming.

As we finished our meal and thanked Agna once more, he told us that the elders had approved our stay and our yurt was primed. We kings had then been travelling in shadows for eight weeks, never afraid yet never at ease, so we were eager to rest and unwind.

As we followed Agna out of the House of Pinecones, so, too, did an informant leave out to report our presence to Natenite authority. Though GAS and the IV had not publicized our descriptions, all knew that their targets were a group of outsiders of superiority. The whispers and attention that our meal had created had provided this hooligan turned informant his next mission. To bear the fruit of chaos and turmoil amongst the only ones who had and would love him, and nurture any and all seeds of division.

After sleeping beneath animal skins and pelts in a warm and luxurious yurt near the homes of Agna and his family, we awoke rejuvenated. As Agna's daughter, wife, and mother made us breakfast, our questions about their colorful culture were eagerly elucidated. They were of the Fire Lords' Tribe, the tribe responsible for fire related Dread duties like sparking and feeding and fighting fires. We were shown the secrets of tinder, oils, long-lasting wicks, and of fire retardants, and we were told their dreams and desires.

Agna's father, Drakon Agni, was one of the last living examples of a *Heruka*, a shaman and magician of the Fire Lords' Tribe. Drakon told us of the greatest Heruka ritual, called the House of Bennu, in which one stays inside a home that is burned, yet emerges alive.

Throughout that day in the Dread village, we experienced the gamut of the cultures and conclusions of the 'called but not yet chosen.' Though they were fire and smoke people, the post traumatic stress of repression and demonization had left them frozen. Some of them had victim mentalities, some were paranoid, some slothful, and most had plans of which few ever manifested. With the growth of GAS and Natenite culture, the growth of Dread culture amongst their youngest generation had become arrested.

Soon, a young Dread greeted Agna and said that he was soon traveling with his associates to see the new station, called a Ventracalis. When we asked Agna, we learned that as the train system expanded, a new arena would be built next to the station for the Spectacalis.

GAS had long been a lover of theatrics and make-up, of drama and dressing up, and he used his new status as a sun sized limelight. In fact, GAS had only ever agreed to play king after his twin cousins and lovers convinced him it would be a grand spotlight. After becoming king, even this was not enough adoration, so his arrogance convinced GAS to become a living god. Then came his ruse as the son of Naten, and his eventual claim that Naten and Amen were now enemies at odds.

Through false flags and terrorist conspiracies, GAS then created a climate in which he could murder the Amen priests in gladiator games. And he concluded every one of these devilish spectacles by performing fake feats of superhuman ability, reveling in his fame.

When we learned that the ice age had begun after the Church of Romilon named GAS their new Christ, our purpose was clear. We told Agna that GAS must be extinguished, and though he agreed wholeheartedly, he begged us not to interfere out of Dread fear.

We kings soon saw what Agna could not, that he and his people were free from GAS only because they were imprisoned in their minds. Systematic efforts were taken to keep them a people 'eating their hearts,' too afraid and ashamed to use their powers and combine. These vicious efforts were never-ending, and coincidentally, just then, the Dread informant was imprisoned, supposedly for his own good. After learning of the soldiers' plans to invade the Dread camp that night, the informant also agreed that it was best he should.

As we kings ate spicy oxtail stew made of the sanctified meat of sacred bulls, one thousand soldiers closed in on the campsite. Biastar asked, "Lord Krstjah, whilst in the bride's bedroom, how is one to begin to see synchronicities as vividly as one sees light?" And Krstjah saith,

> *"Axé, discipline is the key to opening the third eye; the discipline to perform Maat daily despite ridicule and Bad Faith. This black-light blinding is a reminder that the Almighty is the cause of all effects, and the will of the ego must become but a wraith.*
>
> *In recognizing in all things the Almighty, discipline shall become transcendent awareness, noble conduct, and divine acculturation. So in that Cave of Brahma of the pineal, discipline is the cause and effect, and the key to Synchronicity's illumination."*

Suddenly, Agna's brother ran into the yurt yelling of an army of invading soldiers that were rampaging the village on a manhunt. We kings understood that the authorities had been alerted of our presence, and that this invasion came not from coincidence or a hunch.

In the heat of the moment, Drakon created a plan for our escape, and after we reasoned it best, we set out on one accord. As Agna's brother gathered nearby soldiers, and the women located a safe path out of the village, Drakon declared us Fire Lords. Agna said his farewells to his father, and begged him to be safe, and Drakon promised that he would see Agna again someday. Krstjah relieved Agna's concerns and said Drakon would surely make it, for Drakon's transcendent awareness would find a way.

Agna's brethren collected thirty-two soldiers nearby by telling them he had found the fugitives, and then he led them to their yurt. Drakon welcomed the soldiers inside as we snuck out a hidden exit in the back of the yurt and out to the village's outskirts. Once inside, Drakon pointed in silence at piles of animal pelts under quilts, as if to say that the fugitives were there asleep. The soldiers made their way inside like thieves in the night, lining up inside in a battle formation without making a peep.

When they were finally all in, Drakon closed the door behind him and set the door and himself ablaze before the men knew. The holy oil he used made unquenchable fires, and the yurt burned bright all night, as Drakon performed the House of Bennu.

Agna and we kings made it to the old transportation center, where large automobiles gathered and shuttled citizens across the nation. This was the old system now being replaced by GAS' new train system, called Sushumna, which had not yet reached that location. After seeing his father's heroism, Agna overcame his dread, and agreed to escort us to the newest station, the Third Ventracalis. There we would find GAS and his entourage, the new arena of stone which held the Circus Spectacalis, and the newest Ice Palace.

Before we boarded our bus, we kings redonned are priestly robes, and we silenced our minds as we prepared for spiritual war again. We were to be gladiators in the stone arena, and because it was where Amenites where killed, it was called Conarium Foramen.

Our journey there would take three days, over a rough and foggy road, under skies filled with murres and golden eagles. Would only we have sprouted wings in order to fly there, too, for inside the bus we witnessed more of Gidipride's evils.

Amenites could continue their hypocritical and xenophobic culture, so long as they did not publicly condemn Naten and its culture. The Naten way attracted those who had been once rejected, the deplorable and corrupted who now fed on the Amenites like vultures. Whilst on the train, we kings were treated like Agna and the Dreads thanks to our hair, and ignored by the wicked snobs on the bus. Amid the noise, we managed to overhear news of an elderly Dread killing himself along with thirty-three soldiers, despite the ruckus.

Agna was unfazed by this, and he told we kings that he would keep the faith in Drakon that Krstjah had placed in his heart. Agna told us that nothing that Natenites believed they learned from the news should be considered true, for they were unable to be smart.

Through fire rituals, the Heruka had divined that GAS was doing the Evil One's work by spreading not just ice, but also Brain Sand. By poisoning the water and the meat, GAS was slowly corroding the mental capacities of the nation with highly poisonous neurotoxins. The poison worked in conjunction with the civil disharmony and the violence, for fear is the catalyst on which the poison thrives. Agna then told us the final truths which the elder Dreads had divined; truths which, from the Third Eye, GAS could not hide.

After GAS spelled out his plot to consolidate power and become a 'god,' Iset gifted GAS with a mix of monsters and beasts for his spectacles. Wild animals were pitted against beasts such as GAS' favorite two sabertooths, who also acted as executioners in the festivals. What remained of the bodies of the Circus' victims was said to be first blessed by the solar wind god Naten, then respectfully cremated.

However, the fire rituals of the Heruka had helped them divinate that the victim's massacre was only the first time they were desecrated. The bodies were fed to wild animals, which were then sold as 'hot dogs' and concession food to the clueless Spectacalis' fans. Before they were fed to animals, though, the bodies were processed for two delicacies exclusively for GAS; pituitary and pineal glands.

As we neared the penultimate station before our destination, we stayed on high with Dread ganja, which made some passengers vexed. Biastar then asked, "Lord Krstjah, after discipline bestows the sight of Synchronicities in the bride's dark bedroom, what is to come next?" Krstjah saith,

> *"Axé, after disciplined practice, and constantly being grateful, reveal the new sight, one shall open one's own Idi of the Eye. With these new skills, one must face one's own nemesis, which will then uncover itself as the one sleeping in that bedroom in the sky.*
>
> *This nemesis is one's own shadow and antithesis, and often it is the dragons of the past, and these can only be defeated with temerity. For success here shall not hinge upon proper execution during the confrontation, but upon the grace of the Almighty and one's own sincerity."*

While we kings were leaving our bus for a rest break at the penultimate station, the Third Eye of Agna fully opened and he had a vision. As he looked north towards the Ice Palace, Agna Agya Agni saw endless plumes of smoke, as a reality and not as an apparition. Agna then intuited things to come, that a legion of soldiers was waiting for us, and that brimstone and fire were waiting for Gidipride. Just then, a crowned eagle flew to the southwest over us, and Agna knew that we fire lords had providence and would not die. He then liberally anointed us with the Dreads' most sacred oil, which was made from the seeds of a tree that bears eight fruits. He told us that we were now the Fire Force of the Fire Lords, and ready for the bluest of flames in our anointed fire suits.

After our bus started again, menacing military jeeps appeared from the rear, and they escorted us to the final transportation station. Soon, we saw the Ice Palace, and just before it the transportation center, where 1080 soldiers waited for the occasion. Confrontation was obvious, and whilst we kings had long replaced fear with courage, I was surprised to see no fear on Agna's face. Military vehicles of every kind surrounded the final station, and inside, Natenite soldiers and the IV crammed into every possible space.

When the bus stopped, Agna stood and said that we were foreign Champions, in town for the Spectacalis, and that everyone else could safely exit. As the anxious civilians made their way off the bus, a mathematician amongst them counted the assembled IV soldiers to number 666.

As the last civilian made their way off, I in I saw Krstjah's smile widen the way it does before he plays his flute or initiates a fun prank. Krstjah then said that after six years of our protection, it was finally time for him to protect his friends, and I still give thanks! Biastar understood first, and after he told Krstjah that he had always already been protecting us, he kissed Krstjah's burning hand. Zorastar smiled as he lifted and squeezed Krstjah in a powerful embrace, and then said "My demigod has grown up and become a man!"

I in I was deeply saddened, yet I knew in my heart Krstjah would live, and as I kissed his cheeks, my lips were blackened but not burned. Before informing the soldiers that Krstjah was surrendering so we kings would be set free, Agna thanked Krstjah for all he had learned. We kings watched from the bus as Agna spoke with the captains of the Gidipride and IV forces, and we watched as they both came near. They informed us that the offer was accepted, and then the IV captain was given a pair of enchanted handcuffs that Jondes had engineered.

Called the Dragon's Blood Seals, they were Iset's most precious possession, created to mute any psychic abilities in his nemesis and bane. As the captain approached the door, it became like a sun to him, and he was blasted with scorching heat from a fire both invisible and arcane. After his vision faded, and his legs froze, the captain dropped the handcuffs and fainted, and was dragged back into the fold. The Gidipride captain managed to step onto the bus, and he saw three orange flames and one blue, before he, too, fell out cold.

We kings laughed with vigor as he was dragged away, and we overheard Agna volunteer to place on the enchanted restraints. We kings were commanded to exit the bus first, and after doing so, we allowed them to place shackles on us without complaint. We kings were escorted to seats in the stone arena, and surrounded by a sea of soldiers, where we had to listen to them as they laughed and cheered for death. While there, we would overhear them repeat the answer that the IV captain had given after being revived and asked what had happened: "Dragon's breath!"

Agna later told us that after cuffing Krstjah's wrists, the cuffs began to sizzle and smoke until Krstjah lost his red and blue glows. And as he walked Krstjah through the army of soldiers, they lurched away in terror, as if he were the light and they were only shadows.

My lord Krstjah was taken in handcuffs up to the arena's upper room, where that devil of pride, King GAS, was being dressed by young boys. The fancy dressing room was filled with satin and silk and gold-framed mirrors, and GAS was being suited in the tech he used in his ploys. His twin lovers, Jannes and Jambres, were sprawled out on a bed, and they watched as Krstjah was led before the King of Gidipride. When at last GAS turned to witness Krstjah, his antithesis, he was taken aback by Krstjah's sublime beauty, and he became green-eyed.

GAS soon gathered his wits, and welcomed Krstjah to what he called the greatest show on Kismet- the Circus Spectacalis. GAS then said that for Krstjah, it would truly be a show to die for, and the laughter from his sycophants that followed filled the palace.

GAS then admitted that the freezing of his country was no accident, and that Jondes' alchemy was responsible for Gidipride's devolution. Years ago, Jondes created a subzero degree ice-thrower, which used an ice dragon's crystallized heart to generate cold fusion. Iset had given GAS this technology, which he was using to create chaos in Gidipride in order to make new laws and a new order. Iset preferred ice desertification to war, hoping to preserve resources for future exploitation, for Iset was a resource hoarder.

GAS detested Iset's greed, for GAS' vice was not a thirst for endless wealth, but a thirst for endless adulation by obsequious fans. GAS then said that being simply the Christ of the empire was not enough, and that becoming the world's sole God was his ultimate plan. Now fully suited, GAS felt safe enough to stand next to Krstjah, after which he laughed and dismissed Krstjah as little more than a Dread's fire. "It is I," he said, "King Galileo Anero Serapis, and I alone, that is a living god, and I who must be Kismet's Lord, God, and sire."

GAS then said, "Though you are no god, I am going to make you a star, for today you shall be in the Circus' final event. Either you will be willingly beaten in combat by my Gidipride champion, or you will be personally responsible for your three friends' torment." Dressed in his glistening and dazzling suit, beautified with makeup and jewelry, GAS dismissed Krstjah off, like he was a boss. Krstjah was then taken to a special room of the arena, made specifically for the highly dangerous, called the RAS, or 'Radical And Star-crossed."

Soon after, thousands of fans and witnesses were seated in the arena, and a fireworks and drone performance announced the start of the show. The spectacle's brutality would slowly increase, as it began with the murder of animals and had the Trial by Tiger as a crescendo.

First, golden and crowned eagles were released from the arena's grounds, then shot down by snipers with laser-scoped rifles. Next, *19* beautiful black oxen were attacked by *7* gigantic wolves, and the fans delighted in the slaughter of the Amen idols. Then, panthers, tigers, and lions were pitted against gigantic sabertooths, who always tore the noble cats to pieces and shreds. Finally, dozens of lightly armed Amenite families were forced into the arena to face the same sabertooths, and among them was Agna the Dread.

The Circus' Trial by Tiger entailed working with others to successfully kill one of the gigantic sabertooths, and thereby win one's freedom. If you managed to assist in or kill one of the colossal beasts, you could exit the arena with up to *7* others and be exiled from the region.

We kings watched as a snarling sabertooth moved towards Agna and the *19* Amenites surrounding him, and we watched the monster's attack. It killed all *19* there gathered before Agna managed to gouge out the beast's eyes with his bare hands, after jumping onto its back. Arena guards on the sidelines went to take Agna from the arena, but not before offering him the chance to free someone else as well. Agna saw a baby tiger lying unharmed next to its slain mother, and after retrieving it, they were both taken back to the gladiator's prison cells.

Once the bloodbath had ended, bodies were cleared from the arena while the most popular band in the country played its hit songs. Soon, the arena's lights flickered and flashed, and the fanatics began to cheer knowingly, as GAS appeared to the sound of gongs. We kings watched GAS hover above the arena, playing the part of a god, as the attendants cheered hysterically for their god-king.

GAS spoke flippantly through the arena's speakers, and his extreme disrespect of those recently slaughtered was sick and shocking. He joked and grandstanded, and said that those who had died had been judged guilty by Naten and would be holy meat for his pets. GAS then promised the greatest show ever at the Circus, and said that the trial of the emperor's most wanted terrorist was up next.

King Galileo Anero Serapis then proceeded to perform the false feats of superhuman ability which regularly culminated the grisly affair. He invited the snipers to shoot, and when they dramatically took aim and fired on him, the bullets passed through him as if he were air. GAS seemed to disappear, and then appeared to teleport to each sniper one by one and malfunction their weapons with a blue light. In actuality he had activated a cloaking suit, and as holograms were projected at the snipers, GAS invisibly descended out of sight.

Finally, the arena's lights were fully restored, and GAS stood in the arena's center with his two giant sabertooths at his side. He dared anyone who wanted to challenge his supremacy to come forward, but he would remain unchallenged by the citizen's of Gidipride. "And so," GAS said, "on to the main event of the evening, and my introduction to you of the most wanted man on the planet. In fact, I will have you know that the Immortal Vanguard of Romilon here and in neighboring countries are looking for this very bandit."

Krstjah had been led just before the iron gates to the arena, and he watched GAS in the center of the arena and felt ecstasy. On the bus before being detained, my lord Krstjah had already expected a spectacular triumph over evil that all of Kismet would see. When at last the gate opened to the arena's lights and crowd, Krstjah was on the most high vibrations, and felt as if his soul had wings. As Krstjah neared the arena's center, GAS said, "My gift to you, my children, is he that terrifies Iset- that only mortal king of kings."

Suddenly, horns began to blare, and fireworks and confetti filled the air as the crowd again cheered knowingly in frenzied anticipation. As the iron gates opened, and smoke bellowed dramatically into the arena, GAS introduced Kranium Paidexpert, the champion of the nation. He was no more a warrior than GAS a god, but because of his beauty, GAS had given him a nanotech suit of armor to ensure victory. Nevertheless, Krstjah danced and toyed with Kranium during their fight, for the Rasayana is that which is revealed to babes, but to men a mystery.

Finally, Kranium decided to rush Krstjah with such speed that Krstjah would not be able to spin away like a top or a wheel. As Kranium neared Krstjah, Krstjah dodged at the last moment, and he used Kranium's helmet to separate the Dragon Blood Seals.

Krstjah's ecomorphic field was once again free to express, and Kranium began to see and feel the shimmering heatwave aura of my lord. Kranium's courage faltered, and he contemplated surrender, but then he remembered his ego, and the cheers and adulation of the spectating horde. Kranium was certain he would be killed anyway, if he were to forfeit, so he grandstanded to the crowd and rushed forward to deliver a fatal blow. As Kranium neared him, Krstjah's emotions combined into an enthusiastic courage, and he reached a state of calm and flow.

Krstjah's body compelled him to step forward and match Kranium's attack, and their explosive impact sent Kranium flying 7 meters above the ground. Kranium's azure nanotech suit had disintegrated above his waist, and the heat of the explosion had caused his lily white skin to turn brown. The crowd fell all but silent at the sight of their battered champion, and this brought we kings more joy than any praise from men. GAS tried his best, but could not hide his alarm to those with eyes to see it, as he had instructed Krstjah to play along but die in the end.

Krstjah turned to face GAS, which catalyzed GAS' cowardice, so he attempted to force his sabertooths to attack my lord by saying "Sekkem!" The beast were trained to attack on that command, yet they could not step forward to attack Krstjah, for he looked to them like venom. In their eyes, Krstjah went through a transformation to his spirit-animal form, an all black lion with a blazing mane of golden fire. GAS repeated the command over and over again, but instead of listening to him, the sabertooths calmly walked to their dens to retire.

Krstjah then began to speak not only to the citizens of Gidipride, but also to those around Kismet that had tuned in to the wicked debacle. He warned that violent selfishness was a path to hell, and Krstjah offered the crowd GAS' own confession as estoppel. Krstjah spoke to Kismet from that den of sin, and he elaborated how Iset and GAS were destroying the nations with ice. Krstjah then said,

> *"There never was, there is not, and there never will be a sole christ or son of god, for all who walk the Path to Enlightenment may be KRS."*

GAS performed his greatest bit of acting, and laughed off Krstjah's claims, calling him a mad cult member like all of the Dreads. Krstjah detailed the different technological devices GAS was using to seem supernatural, and these revelations finally went to GAS' head.

GAS attacked Krstjah by firing his projected laser ball of blue light, which was a signal to hidden snipers to fire fatal bolts of electricity. But in the *Flow of the Heart*, Krstjah could see the shots coming as if from a god's eye view, and he dance-dodged them with simplicity. This caused GAS to attempt to use the jackal-headed scepter he bore, which could melt skulls and bones like a blazing fire melts ice cubes. As Krstjah easily dodged, GAS demanded that Krstjah reveal the secret to his power too, to all those watching on the tube.

This caused Krstjah to actually consider himself and his power, and he reasoned that his power was thanks to the grace of the Almighty. Krstjah then resolved to dodge fate no more, and as he did *Sun Namaskar* and chanted the Shema Omega, a revealed vision entered his psyche.

Krstjah saw himself in the center of a gigantic ball of fire, and he connected with the feeling of being a sun as if he already were. Suddenly his skin became as hot as a fiery furnace, and the Dragon Blood Seals disintegrated into a smoke which smelled of myrrh.

Suddenly, Krstjah's visual acuity was magnified, and he could see the Sun as if he had telescopic and unlimited vision. In the center of the sun was a boat as large as the *Great Pyramid*, with wheels emblazoned with a star pentagram with golden definition. The boat was drawn by three lion-faced dragons, with red, green, and blue skin, and the sight of their driver made Krstjah introspective. For the driver resembled a bare-chested GAS, and when Krstjah closed his eyes to consider this, he saw the boat from a god's eye perspective.

Krstjah looked down at the boat, which was a massive, stone temple structure, and every temple was unroofed and open. There were ornate statues of the three dragons, and giant statues of a golden and crowned eagle perched on the boat's edges as if to defend. In the center of the boat, Krstjah saw a giant, blue man, with dreadlocks of fire, meditating and floating above a gigantic golden cup. He wore a crystal crown, and while his left hand held a crystal cube topped by a golden pyramidion, his right hand pointed up.

As soon as Krstjah understood that this was his father, the Sun, his father opened his eyes and stared at Krstjah through his flames. Krstjah's projection soon ended, and he was back in his body and in the Conarium Foramen, after his father had uttered his own true name.

Now back in the midst of the roaring crowd, with GAS still attacking, Krstjah understood the vision he had seen with his Third Eye. Krstjah finally answered GAS, saying,

> *"My strength comes from my father in heaven, the Sun and that most high symbol of the Almighty, who is Kairos Ra Stari."*

Upon saying his father's true name, the *Idi of Transfusion* unlocked within Krstjah, and he transformed before our eyes. First, a lightning strike of fire seemed to shoot from the sun and strike the Conarium, and a fire on Krstjah rose high into the sky. A gust of wind then sent Krstjah's fire over to GAS, and he was set ablaze, and ironically condemned by wind and his god, Naten. As GAS burned alive spectacularly, Krstjah spread out his burning limbs and looked to the sky, causing him to look like a *Star-man*.

Then the fire of Krstjah rose over his head, and transformed into a majestic phoenix of fire, before flying above where we were located. When it was a thousand meters above the Conarium, the phoenix stretched out its huge wings and detonated. The explosion incinerated everything in the arena, and a mushroom cloud of steam formed from the evaporation of the Ice Palace. As the steam dispersed, it revealed a ball of fire, like a small black sun, which hung in the sky above the city surrounding the Third Ventracalis.

Kairos Ra Stari, on his boat called the Chakrari, sensed the sun of his son, and again opened his eyes and witnessed his firstborn son. Krstjah's sun brought a smile to Kairos, and he then blew wind and fire from his mouth towards Krstjah, just as the miracle begun. As Crovin circled beneath the sun of Krstjah with crowned and golden eagles, solar wind dispersed his sun's fire throughout the ozone. The fire became a billion *biophitons* of fire, and when these biophitons contacted ice, it created a steam explosion.

When these biophitons made contact with natural fire, they intensified the fire and torches tenfold with an unquenchable flame. In little time, shops and homes and buildings were catching fire, and Gidipridians learned these fires burned until nothing remained. Drakon Agni had secretly coated our garments in the fire repellent used by the Herukas, so we were like him, singed but unscathed. Agna and the tiger were also unharmed, and he gifted Zorastar with the tiger, named Sekkem, when they emerged from their cage.

Krstjah had catalyzed the courage and fire of the Dread people, and they burned away all their shadows with the wisdom of the fire. Krstjah had destroyed the christ of the Empire, and by defeating his current shadow, his EMF and its frequency was free to grow higher.

Biastar later asked Krstjah if what had happened was the result of Krstjah overcoming his own shadow in the bedroom of the bride. Krstjah saith,

> *"Axé, after the climax of the soul overcoming its nemesis, the soul is rewarded with the crown of a sun, and it activates its Idi of the Eye."*

The Dreads were still enraged by the raid on their village, and they took up the everlasting torches as if it was their courage's prompt. In a week red from brimstone and fire, the country and frozen tundra became a bogland of low waters like the *Vasyugan Swamp*.

We kings left Gidipride only after celebrating Krstjah's 7th birthday with the Agni family, when Drakon performed fire magic. Though we celebrated amongst the smoldering ashes of a once grand and decadent land, Krstjah's joyous occasion was far from tragic. As we sat by the fire with the Heruka elders on our final night amongst them, Krstjah vowed to never again hide from a challenge or enemy. We knew this meant confrontation, but we kings had long since been 'For Rastari and I in I until the END,' and beyond infinity.

After bidding the Dreads long life and prosperity, we kings headed east for the land of Romilon and the emperor of lies. As we walked off, just as Agna Agni had first seen us in the midst of heat waves, he last saw us cross the horizon and enter the sunrise.

The Risen Sun

As we kings traveled east over hills and valleys, past plains and over straits, we watched with wonder as Shai Mika-el raised up Sekkem. Again we ventured through a land that resembled a heaven, with majestically flowing green hills and mountains with cloudy rims.

The tops of some of the trees were sun-bleached golden, and the snow-capped mountains in the distance seemed to be striped like a tiger. We lived at the highest elevations in the most high vibrations, in a sea of pure air that perfected our breathing and our very fiber. I in I became high on life, and even a deep breath of fresh air would cause my heart to tingle and my mental frequency to go higher. We kings began to see reality as it is; simply a dream of light and shadow, like the dancing silhouette of Krstjah before the campfire.

At the winter solstice, we arrived at a 7 hundred mile arc of 1005.84 meters high mountains, and we camped on the tallest one. For those two and a half days, Krstjah stared into the sun from sunrise to sunset, as if his father, Kairos, had news to tell his son. We kings stared along as much as our eyes and stamina would allow, but I was often transfixed by a herd of a thousand reindeer. The majestic animals were ever vigilant, and in time I realized why, after I caught a glimpse of a more deadly mountaineer.

A snow leopard and her young son were stalking the herd, and King Zorastar said that the mother was teaching the son how to survive. On our last night on that mountain, King Biastar asked Krstjah to teach us more about the crown of a sun and our personal *Idi of the Eye*.

Krstjah saith,

> *"Axé, past the nemesis in the bed is the Door to the Upper Room, and the soul's new sun and Idis of the Eye are its keys.*

133

The door shall be opened by one's Iyrin, and then one is baptized by a holy and fiery light which shall activate brain sugar and DMT.

The brain will then be set ablaze by Holy Fire, as its stamina and attention increase tenfold and it releases more bioluminescent cells. Thus the brain and soul become enlightened, and one must begin the work of the bodhisattva, as the Path to Herudom unveils.

The soul should then become a bright and shining hero model for those yet on the Path, even if this leads to martyrdom or demonization. For only after one fulfills their ultimate soul service shall they attain their Toll for Immortality, which is the Idi of Solvation."

As Krstjah completed his sun staring feast before the middle of the next day, he began to see the circle of the sun as a shadow and not as a light. His mikarbod was soon drawn into that keyhole of the Sun, and it entered a black void where no thing was in sight.

Suddenly, a tiny atom burst into existence, and as it grew suddenly into a star, a second atom awoke and started creating a second sun. Then Jupiter, the Moon, and the stars emerged, and then a plane of earth appeared just before a battle between the suns begun. Krstjah saw Saturn lose its fusion and become but a planet, and he watched as Kairos was crystal crowned, yet he could not see by whom. Finally, Krstjah saw Kairos watching his birth and granting Queen Omega's wish, and the graciousness of his father made Krstjah as joyous as a bridegroom.

Suddenly, Krstjah heard a whisper in his ear so clear he could nearly feel the wind of the words whisking along the side of his face. This startled Krstjah from his vision, and concluded his sun staring ritual, as his mikarbod returned to his flesh in the present time and space.

Krstjah closed his eyes to appreciate and retain all he had been shown, and he began to feel lively and piquant. Krstjah understood that his father had been and always would be, from the very ancient of days, the Almighty's great regent.

Krstjah now knew that his father never slept, and so was always watching over him, and Krstjah was cleansed of all filial sorrow. He resolved to do as Kairos, to ever perform his soul's duty, and Krstjah saluted the rising sun once more before we left our Kilimanjaro.

We kings continued our travel towards the rising sun for 7 months more, through land which seemed untouched and utterly untamed. Until we finally reached a land of more snow than a thousand Gidiprides, where the blazing heat of the sun had been restrained. On the week of Krstjah's eighth birthday, we camped atop a small mountain, in a cleft of shimmering rock covered in snow. With the last of Agna's oil, a 7 meter rope, and some fire magic, Biastar created a giant wick that burned bright and slow.

We spent Krstjah's birthday enveloped by the glory of the fire and dazzled by the twinkling of the stars above and the snow below. Krstjah wanted only to give gifts on his day, and so we kings fasted and prepared ourselves to receive a great secret he promised to bestow.

Krstjah saith,

"Axé, the story of the ego is, as all things in this realm of illusion, only a momentary figment of the great imagination. We are not these mortal egos and bodies, for we are truly eternal ions, suns, and souls of heavenly generation.

The final goal of the Path of Enlightenment is to identify not as a solitary and mortal self and I, but with the Superself and The I. This is the ultimate soul which is simply simulating our mortal soul incarnations until finally its star shines everlastingly in the 13th dimension's sky.

> *To identify as The I is to identify with all of nature's principles,*
> *with the wind, and stars, and the energy of the Holy Spirit*
> *as you yourself. In intimately knowing and becoming the Holy*
> *Spirit in this way, we awaken the cosmic consciousness and*
> *awareness of the Superself."*

Over the course of the day, Krstjah explained how we would obtain this cosmic consciousness with the aid of our own Iyrin and dreams. For the Iyrin is a messenger from our own Superself, and with its assistance, the soul may be directed towards that which redeems. Krstjah said that our Iyrin would provide the keys to reprogramming our unconscious minds with aids such as prayer and lucid dreaming. Krstjah then told us of the secret ritual called *Gratitude Tuning*, and as he described it, his skin started gleaming.

This ritual was designed to create a metaphysical time-warp, by transforming one's present state into that of a future state. The future state was the state in which you already had your wish fulfilled, and the object desired, and being in gratitude was the key to the magic gate.

Krstjah then told us to repeat and internalize the following *Gratitude Solvation Prayer*:

> *The I in I is the joy and light of the sun,*
> *and I in I am grateful that the Almighty*
> *has given my soul a purpose to fulfill.*
> *The I in I is the truth and power of the One,*
> *and I in I am grateful that the immortality*
> *of my soul is the Almighty's will.*

Krstjah then told us to hum the Shema Omega after performing *Dragon's Breath*, and to meditate on the smiling face of our own Iyrin. He told us what to expect just as it actually happened; that we would go through a door into the astral, just as one does when one dreams. Krstjah then gave us the word that would keep us conscious and lucid in the astral dimension, the whispered word that ended his vision of Kairos Ra. When at last we were through the portal and gate into our access to the astral dimension, we were to say the magical word 'Abrakadjabra.'

I, Sattvastar, did as Krstjah advised, and with my eyes still open, I concentrated on the smiling face of Krstjah, for he is my Iyrin and lord. On his golden locks and shining body did I mediate, until I mysteriously began to see my own blackened face instead of his, which I so adored.

For Krstjah is the Supreme Avatar, the Black Mirror for our souls, the perfect example of an enfleshed Superheru and a Starseed soul.

Suddenly, my Iyrin form before me began to shine as bright as a burning flame, yet the light seemed to project inwards, as if a white hole. Into the light hole was my consciousness and mikarbod pulled, through a spiral of light and dark, yin and yang patterns. Until finally I arrived into a vast and pitch black space that was dimly lit by dots of light, as if I was in an interstellar cavern. I was bewildered and amazed, yet by the grace of the Almighty I was able to remember to speak the magic word as instructed. When I did, a storm of stars lit up the dark dimension, and a new location faded into view, as if it had been digitally constructed.

I was now floating inside a mausoleum for Krstjah, and beneath me was an older version of me just before Krstjah's coffin of stone. That me was crying hysterically, and then suddenly I became that older version of me, and opened my eyes and saw how my blackened Iyrin self above shone. Through tear drenched eyes, I saw that my floating and winged mikarbod was made of a rainbow light, just like Himaraja's soul. I remembered that Krstjah is immortal, that death of the body is merely a stage for the enlightened, and my dream self was instantly consoled.

After saying the magic word, Zorastar was floating over an outside market, and saw his dream self mounted on a horse. Through closed eyes, the dream self witnessed a thief snatch and run, and it gave chase after him with its mace raised to enforce. Suddenly Zorastar's consciousness switched just as mine had, and after understanding the light of his Iyrin self flying above, he instead gifted the thief with the mace.

Biastar had found himself above a crowd of paparazzi outside a black-tie gala, and saw his dream self exit the event with a smiling face. As it was being chauffeured away in a fancy convertible, it witnessed a cult of zealots proselytizing on the street corner. Just as Biastar passed them, his consciousness switched, and he stopped the car and reasoned with them, as a redeemer and a reformer.

We kings were then jostled and stirred from our lucid dreams, and we awoke in the night to tremendous quaking and a thick fog of snow. Krstjah was still meditating and dreaming, and where once there was only a faint glow of orange light about his head, there was now a halo.

For the cleft of rock was a giant granite crystal, and after amplifying Krstjah's power, the mountain had started to transform into a future state. Krstjah was not only dreaming of his Iyrin form and a future state of his, but was fast-forwarding even the mountain to a later date.

Yes, a ripple in time was making the mountain climb, and past the veil of snow I saw us rise as if above all fear and melancholy. At sunrise, Krstjah's vision ended along with the mountain's rise, and it had become the tallest on the continent, and renamed Denali.

Krstjah later told us of his ivista, and that he had again seen Emperor Selassie Rastari meditating alone on a mountain high. The descendant of Krstjah who was to be born two thousand years in the future, who had gone to the mountaintop so he may die. Krstjah had watched as Selassie's light and soul left his flesh, just as Himaraja Melchizedek's had, and then the miracle again began. A strike of black lightning hit the body, and in a whirl of wind, its flesh blackened and locks gilded as it became more than mere man.

Krstjah told us what he finally understood this ivista to mean, and as he did, I was warmed by what seemed a fire hidden in his breath. Krstjah saith,

> *"Through birth did mine soul first come into this world, yet I in I shall return again to Kismet through death."*

As Crovin flew above, we kings soon left that tall mountain, now a giant above every other peak which surrounded us. Yet we never came down from the highest frequency, for the power of the *Gratitude Tuning Ritual* kept our soul fire big and mountainous.

And after hearing of Krstjah's return to this world, Biastar decided that he too would live in a new age, and again be Krstjah's Friend. Years later, Biastar would have his body frozen and hidden, whilst his soul merrily astral projected and did not transcend. Biastar's soul returned to his frozen body thirty-three years before Krstjah resurrected back into this world in Selassie's mount. And it is the wisdom Biastar gleaned from his out of body experiences, and during his second life, which the Testament of Biastar recounts.

PART THREE
The Sanctification of the Kings

Fire Island and The Holy Roller

Axé!
All praises and honor due to the Almighty, to the I in I,
and to the light of this world, Lord Krstjah Sa Ra Rastari,
Son of the sun, hero and savior, emperor and mighty king,
Ever living in our hearts and on Sirius, forever let thy name ring.
Forever protect the righteous and those that know and love thee
Forever let our path towards Herudom be free.
Selah!

Krstjah and we three kings traveled for a year along the coast of a continent, again living where the roaring sea met dry land. The dark green of the hilly coasts was our headrest each night, as we watched the stars meet their reflection on the water at the horizon.

At times, at just the right moment, the movement of white waves across the deep blue waters mirrored that of a cloud in the azure sky. Krstjah was as lively and playful as ever, and it was clear to me that his atonement with his father was the real reason why.

In time, we arrived where the coast ended in high cliffs, where one could only reach the ocean after jumping from the highlands. There we kings could see for hundreds of miles, and we saw just up ahead a region off the coast with hundreds of small islands. Krstjah's eyes filled with wonder as he surveyed the many worlds over the edge, and we soon began to explore some of the isles. There were 440 tiny ones, and they surrounded two large islands that were 330 square miles.

King Biastar informed us that this was the land of the ancient people called the Ijah, whose traditions reached back to the flood. King Zorastar said that the Ijah were notoriously the first pirates in the world, and of all ancient warriors, they were most beloved. We then searched the northernmost islands for months, surrounded always by an eerie mist, yet we found not even a ghost. Finally, we arrived to an island that Biastar knew was inhabited, and when asked why, he pointed to our first sight of a totem post.

As we walked deeper into the isle's forest, it become clear that the ancient Ijah had arranged the isles as one would arrange estates. Thousands of years ago, great care was taken in even the location of the trees of the isles, as the Ijah sought to 'balance' the isle's weight.

We soon came across a small village of longhouses and totem poles, all decorated with striking and mysterious imagery. There were bold and bright color patterns, and dreadful depictions of animals and mystical forest creatures, all in perfect symmetry. We came upon a few dispirited women and children, and they greeted us with bemusement, even though they were reluctant. Unsure if we were truly human or evil spirits in disguise, they kindly took us to their chief so that he could make the *Judgment*.

Deep inside the grand, dimly lit longhouse of the village, we came upon Chief Raven Eagled-Hawk, meditating inside a tent. He wore only an ornate apron and a plumed headdress, and he was enveloped in smoke which smelled of ganja and frankincense. As we approached the entrance of his small hotbox, he gave salutations to our divinity in their ancient and dying language. He, too, seemed clearly deadened, and we would learn that Chief Raven used this indoor tent in order to lament and languish.

His heart was stricken from the traumatic stress of the last two hundred and *20* years of his people's tragic history and present. For the tens of thousands who had for tens of thousands of years lived on the isles had in that time been reduced down to just one percent. The Ijah were the victims of Romilonian colonization, and the few hundred that survived now lived on but a few of the isles. When Zorastar asked how their great warriors were defeated, Chief Raven detailed the horrors of war through a false smile.

First, they were mentally colonized, for the details of their myths were easy to come by, and Romilon used these to deceive the Ijah. Finally, when the Ijah began to see through their deceptions and lies, Romilon used a biological weapon it had extracted from hydras. Chief Raven said that the Ijah were recently given back most of their islands on paper, but now they were too few to use the land. The only place the Ijah were now prohibited from visiting or living were the big islands in the middle, now named Fire Island.

Zorastar was annoyed to discover the Ijah did not yet control every isle once again, and he asked why the warriors had not yet raided. Chief Raven said that the Ijah had stopped visiting those islands long ago, and not because they had been persuaded. The sacred and stolen Ijah totem poles had all been taken there, and Romilonians now held strange, private rituals there around pentacles. Every year, 20 thousand of people would visit the region's Fire Island for two annual, three month long festivals.

These were the rich and famous of Romilon, for it was the Church of Romilon which owned Fire Islands and was the festival's sponsor. Chief Raven then paused before saying that they must be worshipping some devils there, because there were always real monsters. Chief Raven told us that everyone wore masks during the festivals, and this probably allowed real monsters and devils to participate. Zorastar told the Chief that we, too, had encountered real monsters and beasts, yet we had yet to see them congregate.

Chief Raven seemed surprised to learn that we believed him about monsters, and he peered deep into Zorastar's eyes before continuing. He said that the near genocide of his people had not yet ended, and Fire Island was the reason their numbers were still dwindling. Every year, dozens of Ijah women went missing, and there were reports of their screams being heard off of Fire Island's coasts. These disappearances were a constant reminder that the Ijah had once been enfeebled and haunted by their very own myths and ghosts.

The next day, the Ijah people told us of their history, and of legends of their ancestors coming out of the primordial waters. We were invited to their upcoming Fall Equinox ceremony, where initiates would graduate after the honoring of martyrs.

The night of the ceremony, the people painted themselves in red and black, and they wore headdresses and feathers. The initiates of their shaman order had carved a new totem pole, and its beauty and magic was orphic beyond measure. After the post was raised by the light of stars and fires, the new initiates were revealed wearing large 'transformation masks.' One had a green snake's head, which opened like a door to reveal the new adept, and signal that he had mastered the kundalini- 'snake energy'- at last.

After the ceremony, at the end of the night, Zorastar told Chief Raven we were heading to Fire Island, as we watched the firelight. Zorastar promised the chief that we would rid the island of the evils that lingered on here in the Ijah's present and twilight. Chief Raven seemed surprised to hear this, and he sat silently to the sound of crackling wood, until he was moved to tears. For we had not come like the evil spirits that terrorized his people, but instead like angelic heroes, prepared to destroy their fears. Chief Raven then gave Zorastar an iron ring, emblazoned with a hexagram made from two triangles, as protection from all evil. He said the symbol showed the birth of the angelic and invincible one, when the mortal soul converges with the Force-Primeval.

As we approached the southern port of Fire Island the next day, we donned the masks Chief Raven had given us to wear. When we arrived, we watched masked guests merrily depart in luxury boats, and we smelled hints of burning flesh in the air.

Everyone wore masks in four distinct categories, mostly goblins and ogres, as one's mask designated one's sexual preference. The Church of Romilon members coordinating the event wore masks and violet, hooded robes, and behaved in deference. Some members greeted guests as they disembarked, and gave them fairy wands which were said to help one encounter more dead souls. We were then directed past a small section of the island, like the island's tail, which had been fenced off by countless Ijah totem poles.

This was the Festival of the Living Dead, a sixty-six-day and six-hour festive carnival celebrating the transgendered and dead. Festival goers waved wands and burned incenses, and looked to have sexual encounters with not only the living, but also the undead. The alleged goal of the festival was to commemorate those that were killed due to their trans lifestyle, or had died during a surgical operation. Kathol Iset had reversed the Church's lethal stance on the subject decades earlier, and this festival was Romilon's supposed expiation. There were countless places to shop for gifts for the dead, souvenirs, sex toys, and hospitals specializing in castration. The highlights of the festival were reenactments of hell by costumed actors pretending to be souls just freed from damnation.

Though we were masked, we kings again stood out from the crowd, thanks in no small part to our large pet wolf and tiger. Before long, we were approached by large men wearing the same mask and little more, other than a tattoo of a black spider. They revealed their concealed weapons, and then their robed leader, Ifrit Strangio, revealed herself and stepped before we kings. Ifrit was a leading priest of Romilon, a social media celebrity, and an advocate and spokesperson for all transgender things.

Ifrit was allegedly a man who had surgically become a woman, but she was secretly a descendant of Jinn cannibals. Ifrit was a *hemogoblin*, a human mutant whose body cannot produce iron, and so they acquire it from consuming the blood of live animals. During the Festival of the Living Dead, Ifrit supposedly worked with the security forces to imprison wrongdoers and protesters. Those so jailed were said to be released after working off their sentence rebuilding the island, as well as singing vespers.

In truth, Ifrit was in charge of choosing who would be secretly sacrificed each night in the devilish rites held on Fire Island. After draining the victim's blood, they were burned alive in coffins or on crosses, while masked onlookers watched and remained silent. In between the two festivals on Fire Island, Ijah virgins were kidnapped and burned during the Church's rituals to the Evil One. Though Ifrit believed we kings would soon be but ashes in the wind, we soon became the reason the living dead were undone.

Ifrit said she knew we were not actually a part of the festival, and she politely asked that we reveal our true identities. After unmasking, Ifrit's eyes widened in lust, especially for Krstjah and Zorastar, and she called them 'devilishly salacious entities.' She said that we would be treated as sex gods if only we obeyed the rules and were nonjudgmental, and then she asked our names. Zorastar told his name, which made Ifrit pause in bewilderment, and ask if he was King Zorastar, the old wrinkled king of ill fame.

Zorastar saith, "Through Faith, what was old has been made brand new, not by merit but by the grace of my lord, Krstjah Rastari." Ifrit said, "I commend you for having the nerve to show up here, for surely you had to know that this would be where you die."

"It is my honor, duty, and pleasure, to persecute with prejudice, anyone who disrupts the festival, and calls our love 'unnatural' sex. We then learned that, long ago, King Zorastar had exiled or executed transgenders, and had called them nature's rejects. He killed nearly a hundred and 20 all-told, and he had not considered that his name would be infamous amongst the community here. In truth, though, none of us kings considered our past much anymore, for we had long lived only in the present of the 'now,' and without all fear.

Ifrit quickly became incensed as she recounted Zorastar's grim legacy, and her bubbling blood-thirst made her face redden. Her curses and threats moved us not even an inch, though, for the wise man's reactions to the words of the fool are deadened.

Zorastar saith, "I in I sincerely apologize if my actions offended you, because I in I love you, and I in I have learned of my error. I in I thank you for your disrespectful and disgusting reaction, for you have given me a chance to forgive you as well, so all is fair. Through the teachings of my lord and savior, Krstjah Rastari, I in I now know that to judge and condemn is the lowest vibration. So low, in fact, that it is the duty of only the god of the below, the judge of those brought low, who is the king of damnation.

"I in I give thanks for the knowledge that the ego's illusory attachment to the story of its past is the final threshold to cross. I in I am not the sins and guilt of my mortal past, but instead I am a tiny avatar of The I, the eternally self-appointed boss.

"You see, as my wrinkles have been undone by my lord Krstjah, so, too, has my arrogance and condescension become naught. I in I now act from a state of love and constructive criticism, and warn you that your ways are the desolation of your *Lot*. For it is written, what appears to be your own choice, is instead the curse of the karma of bearing no children in one's last life. And, also that this twisted and false choice is rooted in the transition from a sycophantic age to an age where radical is right.

"In this new radical age of self-sovereignty, the hastiness to change has not yet found the organic way it seems. May I tell you now that the simplest way to ensure proper progression in this age is to follow the natural principles by any and all means. Henceforth, know that I in I shall follow the law of love and cooperation, and never judge or condemn another pure soul. I in I shall continue to operate according to the rules of natural living, and know that The I is tolerant of the Whole.

"The Almighty has many means and works in mysterious ways, and can easily differentiate the simply misguided from devils. I in I need only ensure I walk with the righteous and in the right way, and wait and watch as the Almighty judges and settles. And, may I tell you now, the

Almighty can even raise up and quicken even the dead, if by grace they be declared righteous. So then, Ifrit, in order to atone for my karma, I in I shall allow whatever punishment you choose, and expect the Almighty to settle my crisis."

Ifrit said that Zorastar could only atone for his crimes against her people with his life, and was surprised when he agreed. This pleased Ifrit, and she told Zorastar to bid his friends a final farewell, and to cooperate with her men as he was seized.

Zorastar turned to us and chuckled, for he had no fear of execution, and he rubbed Sekkem on the head once more. Before Zorastar walked towards Ifrit, Krstjah bade Zorastar to lean in close to hear him whisper these words of candor:

"Axé, the final stage of the Gratitude Tuning Ritual is also the highest form of faith, and this is called the Divine Assumption.

All doubt in achieving your objective disintegrates when you assume that you are The I, that most holiest of presumptions."

As Zorastar was escorted off by the men of Ifrit, Sekkem's sympathetic whimper slowly transformed into a snarl of fire. We kings had far less concern for Zorastar's safety, though, for we had learned that flesh and blood were simply the soul's pyre.

Well after Zorastar was escorted off, Biastar went off with Shai Mika-el and tracked down where Zorastar was being held. He had been taken behind the heavily guarded gate of the thousand totem poles, where the secret sacrifices and executions befell. Biastar had used his Idi of Telepathy to pass through the secured entrance and obtain the secret passwords required behind the gate. Biastar also obtained the masks and robes of the priests for we kings, and he found out Zorastar was to be executed at eight.

Zorastar was wrapped in alcohol drenched papyrus, nailed to an x-shaped cross, and wheeled to the top of a hill on a stage. Around

Zorastar's feet was drawn a pentacle, an ancient magical symbol which the Church foolishly thought they could use as a psychic cage. The masked and robed spectators of the rite were placed in concentric rings around the hilltop, and I could feel their inhumanity. Unbeknownst to us then, gathered around the stage were the monsters and devils only considered real in the darkest of fantasies.

Through the infinite power of Shekinga, and from the genetic residue of the Jinn from the Age of the Avatars, monsters do still exist. Not only were there psychotic devils and possessed murderers around us, but even satryrs, vampires, and the undead were in our midst.

Zorastar was in the highest of spirits, despite his circumstances, and he sang the songs we sang on the mountain with Melchizedek. The chance to prove his love and faith in Krstjah had triggered him, and it was clear to see that his virility and energy were now at apex.

Zorastar sang out, "Oh Krstjah, give us the power! Oh Krstjah, the new age power! Oh Krstjah, give us the power! Oh Krstjah, we want the power! Yes, the new age power, that was given to the Sun's sons, who are True Believers. Oh Krstjah, give us the power! So the wicked and the liar, shall burn in the fire! So thongs of fire can burn up on them, Krstjah! Oh Krstjah, give us the power!"

And just before a torch wielder lit Zorastar on fire, his frequency raised to the height of a tower, as he recalled Krstjah's words, and began to assume he was the *I Am*, and that he could give himself the fire power.

Just as tinder and papyrus caught blazing fire, King Zorastar gave thanks to the Almighty for the power he was about to unleash. He thundered, "I AM the Fire Lord of the Almighty, lit by the love of Lord Krstjah Sa Ra Rastari!," and then I began to smell hashish.

The fire overcame him, yet he continued to shout rhyming I Am affirmations, until Zorastar entered the Flow of the Heart. As he did, his body began to swell up in size, turning first swollen red, then indigo, until finally he was Herculean and Krstjah dark. And as he grew, a band of light emanated from Chief Raven's iron ring, and it seemed to prevent that finger's mutation. And when the flesh of the other fingers had enveloped the light of the ring, the entire fire fused in transformation.

The fire became a giant tiger's head of fire above Zorastar, and it snarled once before it unleashed a roar heard around the isle. I in I looked over to Krstjah for his reaction to all this, and I had never seen before such a transcendent and overjoyed smile. Zorastar's gigantic head and face then looked identical to the eerie black, red, and white totem pole heads of the Ijah. After its mighty roar, the fire tiger seemed to swallow Zorastar, and this created a tremendous explosion that dispersed the fire.

The cross and stage were disintegrated, and the brolic and blackened Zorastar stood motionless but completely intact. As if from *Uncertainty*, wherever the fire landed, it generated tiny fire tigers, and these vicious little beasts went on the attack. The fire tigers began to ignite all the spectators in attendance; first their robes, then their masks, and then even their heads. As we watched those on fire in turn run around and set others on fire, we kings disrobed and unmasked to reveal our long dreads.

The fire-headed monsters ran throughout Fire Island for the rest of the night, and they rolled the fire across the island's every inch. Yet the fire did not consume that or those which were pure and natural, and caused the foliage on the isle only to pinch. Ifrit had both the *Idis of Intuition and Transfiguration*, and so was watching this all in hiding, in its true, ghoulish, male face. As Ifrit watched and began contacting an escape helicopter, the squawking of the raven of Jewhuti led Sekkem to its hiding place.

Soon after the fire tiger explosion, Zorastar's blackened flesh split down the middle, as if a full body Ijah mask of transformation. From inside the husk of flesh, Zorastar began to emerge head first, and he seemed to wear a golden light-helmet that was as bright as elation.

When he fully emerged from his carcass, the helmet faded away into the sky as bits of light, and this triggered an ivista. I in I saw Zorastar wearing the *Helmet of Victory*, one of the divine weapons of the Principals, and the vision was as clear as Krstjah.

I in I knew then that Zorastar had created a wrinkle in time, just as Krstjah had, and he actually manifested forth a future state. In his *Baptism of Fire*, Zorastar had *transfused* into an avatar of the Principal of Mars, *Adomah Sekkemi*, as Zorastar would again do at a later date.

At sunrise, there were nearly no human figures on the entire island, and there were an abundance of black tailed creatures. There were suddenly tons of raccoons, wolverines, and martens, and the sea was full of orcas with mask-like features. Zorastar now had eyes like a tiger to match his golden locks and his Rastari smile, and he became known as the Holy Roller. Krstjah relinquished Zorastar of his chaperon duties, and Zorastar stayed with the Ijah, becoming the islands' patroller.

During the decade he spent there, Zorastar established a new system of culture and government to prevent the *tragedy of the commons*. He began a fire Faith called Asha, which so emphasized virility and fertility and Ijah repopulation that he was also called 'Chief Brahman.'

We kings lived there in the islands with Zorastar and the Ijah for four years, right at Emperor Iset and Romilon's front gates. In time, Biastar learned of the oldest living animal on the planet, a glass sponge sacred to the Ijah that only lives in one of their straits. Biastar discovered that the sponge, called Hecate, has metaphysical properties, and it can unlock the *Idi of Supersense*. The Ijah people would soon awaken great physical abilities and stamina, until their warrior spirit was again immense.

Fire Island became Zorastar's home, and because beautiful women were always there, it was called the Island of Beauties. And because his followers were also called MOORS, it eventually became known as the

RAS HERU KING

Island Where Moors Be, or the Island of *Moresby*.

Holy Smokes! The Biastar Kachina

Axé!
All praises and honor due to the Almighty, to the I in I,
and to the light of this world, Lord Krstjah Sa Ra Rastari,
Son of the sun, hero and savior, emperor and mighty king,
Ever living in our hearts and on Sirius, forever let thy name ring.
Forever protect the righteous and those that know and love thee
Forever let our path towards Herudom be free.
Selah!

When finally we kings and Krstjah again commenced our odyssey, we had been transmuted by the rich diet of the isles. We were now fully charged, so despite the fact we were now to travel into the belly of the beast, we did so with Rastari smiles.

We traveled southeast into Romilon states and cities, and were always protected from authorities by King Biastar's charm. His wisdom and insight kept us secure and strategic, and though we were RAS wanted enemies, we raised no alarms. We were wise to typically travel in the vast regions of Romilon still untouched by modern tech, such as air conditioning. The land fed us with such spectacular landscapes and magical sunsets that I could feel my EMF overflowing and quickening.

We celebrated Krstjah's fifteenth birthday in solitude, on a red and alien landscape of kaleidoscopic rock formations. Biastar was nostalgic while there, and noted with melancholy that this land showed signs of recent desertification.

Underneath the shadows of still clouds, over rouge sand and stone, we saw less and less green and found ever fewer lakes. We found gigantic white beds of evaporated salt rivers, so white from alkali and salt they were like fields of snowflakes. Strangest of all we saw were triangular shaped rock formations, some huge and some small, and all forming what seemed a grid. Biastar reasoned that these rocks were antediluvian technology, as they all formed the same artificial and peculiar pyramid.

One day, we heard a screech in the sky above us, and then watched a red-tailed hawk fly towards two mountainous rocks. We soon made out dusty figures in the distance heading there, too, and they were the same color as the rocks, to our shock. Biastar reasoned that a gathering of the natives must be nearby, so we followed the red hawk and rouge people and found green grass.

Tucked in between the two rock mountains was a lush valley of green hills and a majestic lake, as if we had reached a paradise at last. There were hundreds of people, and at least twelve different tribes, all distinguishable by the bird feathers each group wore. This was the Autumnal Equinox Festival of the Kachinas, when these tribes convened to honor the gods they adore.

During an equinox long ago, their gods had allegedly promised to return one day, and then flew back to their own stars and moons. The tribes now held this festival every year in anticipation of that return, and they celebrated with dances, ceremonies, and costumes. Special events were held during this time, and the male leaders of each tribe would use the time to have political reasonings. The women leaders oversaw craft-making, graduations, dances, performances, and the trading of seasonings.

We were to find out that the exhilaration present was special this year, and we were told why this might be. Thirty-three years ago, the gods had begun to return again, and many at the festival had reported seeing UFOs again recently.

There was ecstasy and excitement on the faces of all ages, and everyone proudly sported their beautiful bird feather outfits. Their joy was uplifting, for we kings knew that they, just as the Ijah, were repressed by Romilon and labeled as misfits. Despite this, their spirits were as high as their feathered headdresses, and I was spellbound by the feathers of ravens, eagles, and jays. The tribesmen were among their loving and distant relatives, and secret, budding romances were evident under Kairos' rays.

And whilst there were variations in the body types of the distinct tribes, they were all of a red copper complexion. All save the Raven tribe, who had mixed brass skin, as fair as yellow and as dark as indigo-black, amongst their collection. This range of complexion was similar to that of the people of Biastar's homeland, called "the Land of Elephants." His people, too, had divergent skin, at times like gold and at others, as Biastar's skin, as dark as the blackest elements.

Strangest of all, the Ravens even had the same golden and blonding hair and locks, the same as Biastar's tribe. In no time, it was as if Biastar had finally become moored to the ground and serenity again, as if he had found once more his vibe. For as we walked around, and participated in costume making and impromptu performances, Biastar began to dance. He had been decorated with peacock feathers, and as he twirled the Rasayana more vigorously, he soon entered a trance.

As sweat and heat flew from his swirl, air and wind gathered beneath him, and he levitated as if he were light as a feather. Then he suddenly stopped spinning, and began gyrating his limbs as if they were flags in whirlwind weather. When he unknowingly began to dance as he had seen the mystics of the Land of Elephants once dance, Biastar entered the *Trance Dance*. His upper body remained still, as his feet tapped the ground as fast as they could move, until he seemed to glide as he advanced.

In this trance, Biastar began to receive downloads of moving images, images like scenes from some specific ghost's childhood. This ghost had been with thousands of his own people when they had witnessed a UFO arrive one night and land in the nearby woods. Just as Biastar saw visions of the ghost's first sight of the grounded and opening UFO, a raven's croak ended his trance. Unbeknownst to him, a crowd of nearly one hundred and *17* tribesmen had come to watch him, and as he ended, a jubilant ovation rose up for his dance.

Biastar was now a *Star*, and word of his dance would spread across the festival, but only one person approached him after the cheer was done. The chief of the Raven tribe was called Hogon Algonquin, and beneath his raven headdress was skin blackened by the sun. He warmly praised Biastar's inspired performance, but when he heard the name of Rastari, his heart suddenly went cold. Hogon turned to leave from us, but he was frozen in place when Biastar repeated a few words that the vision had disclosed:

"Koyaaniquatsi, the ancestors lost their balance and harmony," said Biastar, with his eyes closed, as if still in a daze. Hogon turned immediately and asked Biastar how he knew these words, and Biastar then explained his visions to our amaze. Hogon was baffled by these strange glimpses, and despite sensing that Krstjah was a 'most wanted,' he overcame his doubt. He invited us to a special kiva, where he and other chiefs and elders would discuss, among other things, the increasing drought.

The kiva was built in the traditional style, into the nearby red sandstone cliffs, and was entered from the top by a ladder. A whirlwind of smoke met us as we crossed that threshold, and I only saw the august group gathered after the holy smoke had scattered.

There were eleven wise elders already present in the small room, smoking from ornate pipes around an enchanted object. It was a large, and lustrous human skull made of rainbow aura crystal, like my japamala, and it sat on an obsidian pedestal that was diamond bedecked. We marveled at the dazzling object, we listened as the chiefs reasoned, and we inhaled a medley of rare smokes. Hogon soon asked Biastar to speak more on his visions, but first Biastar had to prove his words were no hoax.

Biastar said, "In truth do I in I speak, from love and for harmony, for Krstjah has revealed to me the way of uprightness. If only I in I had more to share I would, yet my brief abilities of insights were surely only a reflection of Krstjah's brightness."

In time, I in I reached my smoking summit, and as Biastar bravely continued to partake, I saw him again enter a daze. His unblinking eyes stared half-opened at the crystal skull, and his right hand began to draw a *shri yantra* figure as he gazed. Biastar began to have a vision, in which the smoke from the room fused together, and then lifted up the crystal skull until it floated. As it rotated to face Biastar, the skull began to fill with an intense white and blue light, and when it was filled, it unloaded.

The light shot out as a laser beam at Biastar, and it charged and filled his biophotonic aura, until it shone a turquoise light. The light suddenly split into a thousand bits, which then reconfigured into a shining *metatron's cube* that was connected to Biastar's heart like a kite. In each of the 13 circles of the cube, Biastar saw a different series of moving images, all telling a short story, as if a movie. As he watched the screens, Biastar mysteriously heard the singing and rattling of a shaman, and he found it familiar and soothing.

One of the circles showed the UFO arrival he had seen while dancing, and the other circles depicted similar scenes. After the arrival, the UFO had opened to reveal humanoids in snake and fish-headed costumes who had concocted an ET scheme. They pretended to be from the stars and moons, and claimed their goal was to share their knowledge with the people and give them technology. In truth, these were degenerated humans who, after being trapped underground for ages after the many floods, had developed a reptilian psychology.

These humanoids began their plot by sending their ambassadors, who then infected the leaders of nations with parasites. These parasites eventually created an internal negative will, making one doubt one's natural emotions, intuition, and insights. The humanoids gave the leaders new technology, only after they were duped into teaching their people inverted forms of their own traditions. The leaders soon enforced the new inverted philosophy, and the humanoid messengers are made 'gods' in the new superstition.

The domestic animals were infected with the parasites, so that all of the meat eating people developed the parasitic menticide. The nation soon enacted self-defeating policies, which led to drought, lawlessness, tribal war, and ultimately cultural genocide. In the final circle, Biastar witnessed the few survivors which remained forced to live in dangerous cliff dwellings just to escape civil war. Biastar then understood the truth of the 13 circles, just before the vision was interrupted by the croak of a raven at the kiva's door.

He knew that this was no hallucination, and that he had been given access to the *Akashic* records in order to speak the truth. Yet Biastar had long ago promised himself to avoid telling others uncomfortable truths, after a tragic event in his youth. Despite this, the veracity of his vision, and Hogon's earlier request to hear more, compelled Biastar to unmask their gods. He told the chiefs that their gods were actually just wicked and deformed humans, whose otherworldly provenance was mere facade.

And it was as Biastar had always feared, for the elders there were all outraged by his assertions, and called Biastar disrespectful. Hogon managed to quiet the room by stating that forgetting to ask the name of the messenger's god would be neglectful. Biastar restated that he had discovered divinity incarnate and his own Iyrin and angel through the deeds and love of Krstjah.

"Through the love of Krstjah, I in I can see with The I in mine very heart," and then after a pause he said, "Aum Shantistar." And suddenly the elders stared in silence, unable to recall how they knew those words due to the parasite's induced cacophony. Only Hogon faintly recalled the song, once sang long ago during the kachina festivals, called the Blue Star Kachina Prophecy:

> The day of the blue star kachina starts at night,
> When the stars are all hidden by holy smoke.

Then a fiery comet blazing with a blue light,
Shall bespeak the new Burning Age has awoke.
Shanti Shanti Shanti
Shanti ishta Shanti,
Shanti shanti Shanti
Koyan naga Natsi
Shanti Shanti Shanti
Shanti ishta Shanti
Shanti Shanti Shanti
Asta naga Nappi
The day the blue star kachina falls to the land,
Brilliant and on top of a golden house of fire,
The old gods shall be unmasked as The Man,
And this disharmonious age shall become pyre.

This song was given to them by the earliest ancestors they could remember, and seemed to describe the birth of the new age. It was taught that this described angels who fought devils, but the people thought this meant alien contact nowadays.

Soon after Biastar's words, the reasoning came to a close, and Hogon asked us to consider his tribe our own safe haven. He commended Biastar for his courage in relaying the message he was shown, and then Hogon called us honorary Ravens. And just before we rose up the kiva's ladder, Chief Hogon told us that one of their gods was scheduled to appear tomorrow. Despite the parasite's paranoia, he invited us to meet their god, yet he wondered past midnight if we were to bring joy or sorrow.

As the *Harvest Moon* shone bright in the sky that night, Biastar asked Krstjah to explain the visions he had earlier been given. Krstjah saith,

> *"Axé, iman was granted a glimpse of the Intelligence of the Heart thanks to becoming an Akashic magician.*

*After the third Baptism, that of Light, one's Idis of the Eye shall
fully manifest, and the soul's enlightenment shall find refuge in
the heart."*

Before the flickering flames of our small fire, King Biastar then
recounted to us his story, and the origin of his telepathic charm and
smarts.

Surprisingly, his was a heavy heart, for when Biastar was but a
young and new king, he foresaw an age of drought to come. Yet when
he warned his trusted officials, they rejected and ignored his mitigation
ideas due to concerns over their incomes. Only after a third of his
people were either displaced or deceased were Biastar's plans
implemented, and his nation finally secured. Yet Biastar's heart had
never recovered from the rejection of those set in their ways, nor the
tragedy his nation endured.

Wise Biastar would go on to master the art of persuasion and the
ability to motivate and influence, and he even awoke his *Idi of Charm.*
Yet he was never as charmed as he could make others, and his smile
was truly only large enough not to raise alarm. Biastar had learned
that over-empathizing and over-sharing with those set in their ways
could be painful and ill-advised. Yet, that night before the fire, Biastar
understood that he could no longer go on withholding his wisdom and
leaving his heart compromised.

Biastar declared, "From this day forth, I in I shall divulge the good
and healing truth, and ensure mine vibrations remain high. For even
my lowly self, I in I can heroically love, all through the love of Krstjah
in mine heart, as he has ordained I."

Biastar understood then that he need only be himself the
appropriate form of good and uprightness required at any time. This
freed him from judging the merit and intellect of others, and unlocked
the compassion in him that had been undermined. Krstjah's love for
Biastar had become for him the only credentials he needed to feel

fully worthy, at ease, and wholly divine. It was then that Biastar fully understood his own I-Amness and his connection to The I, and then when he began to shine.

As Biastar's smile widened and expressed true joy and bliss, he attuned with the feeling of being loved by Krstjah and eternally Solved. He tuned his gratitude to the version of himself that had already performed his soul's duty, and gave thanks that it was resolved.

And suddenly, his pineal gland began to vibrate at the highest of frequencies, generating bioluminescent photons and light. The cave in his brain became as bright as a *Star*, and a waterfall of galactase and light flowed down and made his heart bright. The light became turquoise as it flowed out from Biastar's solar plexus and surrounded him, until he had an aura like Krstjah. Biastar's Gratitude Tuning had crystallized his DNA into 13 strands, and he now shone blue with bliss as bright as a *Star*.

In those highest of mental frequencies, Biastar truly connected with the egoless I-Am awareness of the entire local space. His mikarbod seemed to float above the area, yet he could instantly be anywhere and anything his attention embraced. As Biastar's mikarbod observed the area, he became aware of the raven of Jewhuti, and then the raven was psychically aware of him. Biastar went in closer to connect with the raven's awareness, and then was given an ivista and the raven's name – Crovin.

Biastar then saw images of himself and with we kings as Crovin had seen us at every key moment of our long journey and odyssey. He saw Crovin on Queen Omega's windowsill that night, and then he even saw the announcement of Krstjah's advention by IT, Jewhuti.

Biastar then understood Krstjah's supreme identity as never before, and his astral body returned to his still shimmering flesh. Biastar then appreciated how privileged he was to be Krstjah's friend, and he would for evermore feel too blessed to be stressed. Biastar could feel how he was but an ion of the Almighty, and was grateful that he had a part to play in the unfoldment of divine will. Biastar's new smile and glow remained with him still to this day, and listening to the *Intelligence of the Heart* became his greatest skill.

Biastar learned how to ask his heart questions, and would receive an intuition or impression of the truth in nearly every case. And thusly, he soon realized that we should rest, so that we were all charged up for the morrow and the events that would take place.

The next day was the Equinox, and the Raven tribe gifted we kings with colorful and striking kachina costumes for the event. Hogon had personally adorned Biastar with raven feathers on his arms and ankles, and in advance, Hogon had given Biastar his consent. As the red copper people gathered in a flat amphitheater made of the area's red rocks, they resembled a herd of a thousand mighty bison.

Soon after we kings took our seats just before sunset, a gray UFO shaped as if a bell atop a shield, appeared on the horizon. The very top and bottom of the craft spun in opposite directions, and a row of lights and windows decorated the midsection. After the UFO had landed 100.584 meters from the stage, and as the crowd began to cheer, the sanctification of King Biastar met its inception.

After the spinning and lights of the craft had ceased, a door opened, and both a metallic plank and a fog lowered to the earth. Soon, four twelve feet tall, blond, shirtless, men and women descended the plank, carrying a crystal palanquin with a berth. The four doors of the ark were made of an alluring silver plasma, which mysteriously flowed and shimmered like liquid smoke. As the giants neared and ascended the stage, they were welcomed by the feverish cheering and weeping of the copper folk.

When finally the giants stood on the stage, the doors of the ark became holographic images of a spacecraft voyaging to our world. After the holographic craft landed, the plasma doors vanished, and out flew a hundred and *17* birds and the herald of the 'alien' peril.

For inside the palanquin sat Parah Sitenoia, who wore a gray synthetic suit like skin, and an enormous helmet with two big, black eye-slits. He was a member of the deceptive humanoids called the Umanaintapy, who were degenerated humans just like evil Ifrit. Parah descended from the 'Umans' that called themselves the Sheti, and they claimed to come from Phoebe and Saturn. Their skin was an albino gray, and they had large, blue eyes, and they were among the first Umans to surface from the caverns.

A millennium in the shadows and in cannibalism had mutated them into a new species, one bent on domination. And they used the ancient and advanced technology that had fallen beneath the earth in previous floods for their abominations.

Generations with no sun mutated the Uman's melanin into a magnesium, so they all were one of fifty shades of gray. Generations of cannibalism infected the Uman with the most extreme of parasites, and of them all, koyan was the worst of the fray. The koyan parasite could paralyze even the mind of its victim, and worked to create its ideal inner ecosystem, one of chaos and anxiety. It could even emit destructive resonances at a molecular level, and could give some of the Umans the ability to hypnotize the elites of society.

With the koyan and antediluvian technology at their disposal, the Uman across the world had secretly deceived humanity. For centuries they had pretended to be from out of this world whilst causing the ruination of nations through insanity.

Parah then clapped his hands and a team of birds lifted him into the air, and carried him through the air by flying beneath his feet. Parah soared as if a windsurfer around the amphitheater, and as he passed the different tribes, the birds of their feather would take a seat. After this spectacle, he was flown to the top of the ark, where he landed and accepted the exultations of the large multitude. After he was given a microphone and the crowd finally silenced, Parah placated the red copper peoples with bird jokes and platitudes.

He continued his ruse as the ambassador of gods living on the moon Phoebe, and vowed to continue to provide their protection. Parah then introduced a new project designed for their good and safety, and said they were all to have injections. Parah claimed to be able to travel into the future, and stated that a terrible and deadly disease would soon begin to infect them. He claimed the majority of them would die in less than *17* years, and then claimed that the gods had created a vaccine to protect them.

As some among the people applauded and thanked the gods, Parah told the people the steep price of their new, special shots. They would have to sacrifice the holiest of regions in all of their culture, a paradisaic region called the *Four Corners* Spot. This land had been ordained as a communal land, where every tribe's ancestors could reside, and it was essential to preventing war. Though the red cooper people all knew of this importance of the Four Corners Spot, Parah's announcement was not met with protest or uproar.

Only Hogon Algonquin stood when no one else would, and he thanked Parah for the medicine, before asking for another way to pay. Hogon reminded Parah of the region's central importance to their culture and unity, but he promised to listen to the gods and obey.

Parah asked if anyone else felt the same, and though they murmured and moaned amongst themselves, none dared question the gods. Parah then told Hogon that this deal had been approved by Emperor Iset, so the likelihood of renegotiating was against the odds. Hogon turned to the other chiefs, and when he saw no resistance to the plan on their faces, he bowed his head in acquiescence. He then presented Biastar and I, and said we were disciples of another living god, Krstjah, who was now in our presence.

Parah was bewitched by Krstjah's beautiful face, and assumed Krstjah was a cyborg created by Umans, like the four giants onstage. He welcomed us and asked us to come up, even though he secretly assumed we were trying to take his territory, and was becoming enraged. Biastar went up on our behalf, and as he did, a cheer rose up from the audience as they realized that he was the dancing peacock. Parah was first surprised by their cheers, but soon grew envious of Biastar, and he felt disrespected when the cheers did not stop.

Parah assumed Biastar had hypnotized the crowd with koyan, and he asked Biastar if he, too, was one of the 'godly watchers.' Biastar said, "The righteous are all but fractals of the one god, yet those who profit from claiming divinity are but impostors.

"The Almighty has given each of us an equal measure of divinity, and the righteous need only be aware of the Almighty within. We are, all of us, light beings tuned to a specific frequency, and we need only express our true tune for the Good to begin. We must again remember the conductor, the Almighty, the great partner of us all, and begin to sing again our natural melody. I in I have found again my natural song, all thanks to the wisdom and grace of Krstjah Rastari, the avatar of the Almighty.

"Through the brilliant love of Krstjah in my heart, I, even I, am a herald of the true and good Almighty inside us all. Everyone here under the sound of my voice, and I, yes, even I, am as godly and divine as mine soul can imagine and recall. Yet words alone cannot express the joy and bliss which the Almighty has given me, so permit me to fully express my melody."

Biastar crossed his arms over his heart, and as he twirled, he unfurled his arms until they were spread and he was dancing with levity. Krstjah was overjoyed by Biastar's praises and performance, and as he began to play his flute, Biastar danced the Rasayana. Krstjah's flute rang out loud and clear, and as the people joyously mimicked Biastar, they resembled choreographed fauna. And soon after Krstjah began to play, Biastar's body heat index rose to a boiling point, and the Hecate and Soma in him coagulated. And there for all to see, Biastar improbably became superconductive and electronegative or simply just magical, and he levitated.

Biastar calmed his frantic dancing and gracefully embraced this zero gravity, and he soon began to hover near the cyborg's heads. For *17* full seconds, Biastar danced the Rasayana in midair, with only hot wind beneath his feathers and golden dreads. When finally he landed and bowed, the amazed and thunderstruck crowd cheered fanatically, using the birdsongs of their tribes. Parah had never made the people so joyous and reverent, for despite his theatrics and the koyan, they unconsciously loathed his vibes.

Parah's devilish vanity had been triggered by Biastar, yet he pretended to applaud Biastar, and thanked him for his dance. Parah then acknowledged our 'otherworldliness,' and started to call us his angelic brothers, yet he never had the chance.

King Biastar interrupted him and said, "There is nothing otherworldly in me, neither in you, but that iota of the divine I in all of us. And yes, in even you and your devilish people, this iota of the Almighty is present, yet you can hear it not amongst your ruckus.

"My friends, it was this I of the Almighty in me which has revealed unto mine eyes the evil and twisted ways of these false gods. For though they told you they came from the stars above, it was the bowels of the earth which produced this cross and fraud. Parah, and Cool-Con Crew before him, are messengers of mutated humans from underground, ones called "Napi" in your prophecies. They have come up to our world to steal and poison and invert, and they caused the death of your ancient people, the Anasazi."

Parah was flabbergasted by Biastar's revelation, but managed to compose himself before calling Biastar a conspiracy theorist. While most of the crowd was stunned silent by these words, a jeer seemed to rise up immediately from the most infected purists.

This involuntary cry against the intentions of the Umans was a symptom of the koyan, for it could create in its victim devastating internal noise. These dissonant and destructive resonances were experienced as subconscious and physical pain, and led to the loss of all calm and poise. So, too, did the jeers of the disagreeable arouse the koyan and its noise in the infected, and the crowd quickly grew biased against Biastar. Just then, Crovin landed on top of the crystal palanquin, and when it croaked, its supernatural voice could be heard from afar.

Crovin now had all golden eyes and feet, and its long cry was at once that of a raven and that of a thousand angelic voices in harmony. This instantly placed the minds of everyone gathered into the epsilon brain state, and it put Biastar's mind into the lambda frequency.

Whilst a sudden blissful drowsiness swept over the amphitheater, Biastar began again to hear and see the 'songs' of the sandstone. For the crystals in a locale's rocks record the auric residue of a space's historical events, and these Akashic records were what Biastar had been shown. As he did, his mikarbod again projected up from his body, higher and higher into the sky away from the motionless crowd. When he had flown so high that we all appeared as ants, Biastar's mikarbod began time-travelling, after vanishing into a cloud.

In that astral dimension just beyond physical time and space, Biastar witnessed all of the key moments of the Uman race. Across the globe, the backwards Uman had come across ancient technology that had been built to go to war, not space.

In the Age of Avatars, supernatural brilliance was not uncommon, and unimaginable technologies were created to fight the Jinn. Some of this survived the World Flood and flowed down below, and when found, it gave the Umans tools far beyond their intelligence. Over centuries, the Uman learned to use this advanced technology, and they used nanotechnology to reverse engineer more. For the next few centuries, they fought amongst themselves for supremacy, and only then surfaced to Kismet in a state of war.

Though the number of their spaceships and cyborgs and soldiers are tiny in comparison, the Uman can destroy any human army. For centuries, they hid and fed on dinosauric behemoths and leviathans of the sea, and only flew over towns when the skies were stormy. Their skin quickly becomes cancerous under the light of the Sun, so they soon created robotic suits in order to come forth by day. They used these suits to observe and confuse humans at first, but then they used the suits to subduct a select few from the fray.

The Uman long ago began experimenting on humans, like laboratory rats, and they could erase the abduction from a victim's mind. They chipped, x-rayed, gene spliced, and mutated human victims, until they created offspring that could interbreed with mankind.

Across the globe, countless groups and cultures had documented sightings of the Uman, and had foolishly made 'gods' of these devils. And soon after the Uman managed to spread their inversion of morality, these societies would collapse, as the Uman and koyan reveled.

The Uman have been recorded as fish or serpent headed gods, or teachers who came from the Pleiades or rose from the sea. For their spaceships were often seen emerging from lakes and off coasts, for there you will find underwater docks which lead to their cities. Once their half-human offspring worked its way into a nation's aristocratic families, this sounded the nation's death knell. The latest and greatest of these aristocratic mixes was the mother of Emperor Iset, the three-fifths Uman named Queen Jezebel.

By the time of Tessarasa, the Uman had the technology to create drones and even satellite space-stations with which to spy on their victims. As emperor, Tesarak Iset discovered the hidden Uman not by intelligence agencies, but through the vibration of their maledictions. Tesarak discovered that the Uman are the world's greatest gold collectors, for they used liquid gold to ease the pain of their afflictions. Though the Uman believed they used the parasites, it was the parasites which used and ravished them, so gold was their addiction.

Whilst they stole the gold of the people, the Uman would invert the people's Faith, until poisoning was called the medical practice, and gold was called gaudy. Whilst Biastar astrally projected through space-time, his sight became visions sent out across the theater and into everybody.

And suddenly, Crovin croaked again, and all gathered there were again conscious of the present, and they all now know the truth. The elderly chief of the Eagles then remembered the prophecy, and the unmasking of the old gods, and he was filled with youth. He cried out, "It's true, it's true, and everyone here with goodness in their heart knows that this is the fulfillment of prophecy!" Parah understood the murmurs of the crowd were now vehemently against him, and assumed Biastar had used technology.

Parah then turned to the elders and spoke in Paradiax, the doublespeak language the Uman used to mind control infected elites. However, the croak of Crovin had re-attuned the ears and hearts of the elders, and their lack of reaction spelled Parah's defeat. The Umans were creatures of war, and even the slightest threat could excite blood-lust in them, so Parah was now truly enraged. He spoke again in Paradiax, now to the infected birds, and they immediately rose into the air in formation like a brigade.

The birds attacked and surrounded Biastar, and began to lift him into the air as they tore at his costume and the raven feathers. Biastar calmly attuned himself to being thankful for just having been freed from them by some mysterious change of weather. And just then, a violent gust of whirling wind flew over the valley, and the whirls were improbably strongest near the stage. Biastar and the army of birds were jiggled and wiggled, and the wind only calmed after Biastar was freed from his birdcage.

The crowd cheered triumphantly, for they could sense that Biastar's improbable magic was different than Parah's technology. Biastar had reminded them of the powers and abilities in us all, which their ancestors were said to have had in their mythology.

Parah realized that the people would soon seek revenge on him, and he boarded his ark and ordered the cyborgs back to his ship. As Biastar looked on, he was given an ivista of the doors of the Crystal Palace of Jewhuti in Shambhala, as if it were a filmed movie clip. Biastar then remembered what he must do, and he rushed to Parah's ark and jumped in through the plasma door. The night before he had prepared himself for the House of Bennu Fire Lord ritual, and when he initiated it in the ark, he became truly MOOR.

The explosion Biastar created ignited the nitrous oxide stored beneath the palanquin, and this created a rocket thrust of blue fire. Crovin flew over to Krstjah and I, as the cyborgs were blown offstage and the crystal ark of Parah rode the blue pillar higher. As it rose and heated, the ark emitted a brilliant rainbow light that grew ever brighter and ever more thick with dimensionality. The ark finally stopped rising when it was high in the sky, and for thirty-three seconds, it stood still as Biastar again left this reality.

Again in the lambda brain state, Biastar's mikarbod was projected in a blitz of images through all of his former soul incarnations. When his mikarbod returned, Biastar's aura burst forth the dark blue light of the cyanolyca, and the ark exploded from this detonation.

The inter-dimensional light grew as bright as the sun and as large as the moon, as Biastar was pushed out through the roof of the ark. The ark then became a Tesla coil, and its arms of deadly plasma began to crash all around the amphitheater, until it tore the stage apart. Parah was disintegrated inside the Tesla coil ark, just as one of the plasma arms happened to reach out to the UFO and ignite its warp drive. Suddenly, a bubble of rainbow light surrounded first the UFO, and then the entire area, as the wind swirled, rocks quaked, and the earth began to slide.

The ship had created its own gravitational field, and this began to tilt everything in the bubble, even the theater and the bedrock. When what was once flat was now huge sandstone boulders jaunting out of the earth at an angle, the bubble of light and UFO vanished into a dot.

Biastar descended on a cushion of smoke, as a tremendous current of wind and purifying hydroxyl radicals swept across the land. The theater, the stage, and everything that was in that bubble was now tilted forty-four degrees, as if by divine plan. Biastar now had wings only around his wrists, elbows, and ankles, and he landed on the remainder of the burning ark with a smile. With his magical blue glow and the waving feathers, Biastar was like a Kachina standing on a house of fire with grace and style.

He would become infamous for that moment, and they would call him the Biastar Kachina, Holy Smokes, and the Blue Monarch. The theater would go on to become famous for its unique design and rare acoustics, and is today called the *Red Rocks* Park.

Biastar's projection through all of his previous incarnations, and through the final one to come, had evermore transformed him. He had activated his 13th cranial nerve, his brain and heart rates were now synchronized, and he had redeveloped the Jacobson's organ. Biastar's heart now had the access codes to the information in the astral network, and he could smell the goodness of things. He now had the *Idis of Akashic Access and of Improbability*- aka magic- so Shaman Brahman Heru Biastar is known as the *Alchemists' King*.

The jubilation festival and thanksgivings for the 'Biastar Kachina' would go on all night, and Biastar cherished the acclaim of proud Krstjah. With Krstjah's blessing, Biastar would remain with the red copper people, and he created for them a spiritual society called Shantistar.

Biastar became, for them their prophesied teacher from the stars, and he taught them the ways of Rastari, and the love of Krstjah. He taught them his Charm, and with it, they became beloved by Romilon's youth, who soon made Shantistar musicians global superstars.

Biastar also taught them how to develop the Jacobson's organ, and with it how to inspect food and spaces for parasites. He taught them how to kill the parasites with spirit baths, where one uses tuning forks while in hot springs and envisions paradise. It was Biastar who wrote the Shantistar Codex, and he who created and distributed the psychedelic substance called KMT. And from these different catalyzations, Shaman Biastar, Holy Smokes, set in motion his heroic part of Krstjah's victory.

The Passion of the Holy Ghost

Axé!
All praises and honor due to the Almighty, to the I in I,
and to the light of this world, Lord Krstjah Sa Ra Rastari,
Son of the sun, hero and savior, emperor and mighty king,
Ever living in our hearts and on Sirius, forever let thy name ring.
Forever protect the righteous and those that know and love thee
Forever let our path towards Herudom be free.
Selah!

Krstjah and I lived there with the Cooper Tribes and Shaman Biastar for 22 moons, in the very heart of Iset's own nation. Never once did we need fear raids or for the lives of our hosts, for we had both their absolute loyalty and Biastar's precognitive information.

Every month, we three kings moved to a different one of the 13 tribes, and we coincidentally left only just before Romilonian authorities arrived. We witnessed the purification of the indigenous folks, and the renewal of their Faith, and we were not surprised when they began to thrive. The empathetic youth of Romilon began to identify with the new Shantistar culture, and they rejected Romilon's evil quiddity. And even more Romilon citizens were introduced to the Shantistar way through the growing popularity of the KMT, also called Lucidity.

After his seventeenth birthday, Krstjah decided to continue his march towards the capital of Romilon, the home of Emperor Iset. We bid Biastar and Shai Mika-el farewell, and traveled east with a group of Shantistar musicians who were performing across the continent. Never before had we traveled with friends, and never before had our travels been filled with such camaraderie and festivity. Krstjah adored the many forms of their tribal music, and I in I often danced beside him to the expressions of their fire and creativity.

The Romilonian audiences were small, yet filled with sincere people who were truly elated to hear great music that was not also heartless. I was amazed to see Romilonians ecstatic from righteous lyrics, and I understood that there is the hope of good even in the heart of darkness.

One night, under the starry light of the new Cold Moon, I had an intuition which disturbed me down to the depth of my very heart. I intuited that my journey beside Krstjah would soon end, after Krstjah achieved the victory assured to him from the start. As I grew sad, I remembered my mountaintop dream of my shadow and Iyrin self, and I recalled the wisdom I had then understood. I recalled that Krstjah, like the memories of our ancestors, lives on with us forever in our hearts, if we but remain faithful and good.

By grace, I in I then lovingly recalled my father, whose early death had long ago caused me tremendous suffering and pain. I then resolved to cherish every remaining moment with Krstjah and my loved ones, and then I remembered my uncle lived in the domain. When I informed Krstjah of my intention to visit my uncle, Krstjah agreed that it was time my family knew I was still alive. Though we kings had long ago agreed to remain undead after the Council of 13 Kings, I longed for my family to know I had survived.

Locating my uncle, Lord Binah Adani Sattvastar, was simple, for he was the owner of one of the wealthiest companies in Kismet. Lord Binah had come to Romilon before my father had died, and his small iron business had become the world's largest conglomerate. Lord Binah had been a wise and kind uncle when I was young, and I hoped that he still had understanding and compassion. However, after I contacted my uncle to let him know I was alive and visiting, he then contacted Iset, and Iset contacted his best assassin.

Yet my only fear at that time was to fail to ask my Lord Krstjah for the essential secrets of his wisdom before we parted ways. Whilst we traveled to my uncle's headquarters, Krstjah revealed to me the final steps in the Path to Enlightenment, in a total of four days. Krstjah saith,

> *"Axé, after one is crowned a sun by the Iyrin, the soul shall begin its unique Path to Herudom and Atonement. When the soul assumes it is The I and experiences its I Amness, it shall achieve the Baptism of Light, and reach true enthronement.*

> *The soul shall then receive the Idi of Nirvana, and the Intelligence of its Heart shall awaken its ultimate abilities and intuitions. In time, the soul shall meet its Neter- the Principal that one's Superself most emulates- and find one's Sanctification Mission."*

Then, the night before we met Lord Binah, Krstjah taught me the final and absolute form of faith, beyond Assumption and Gratitude.

> *"Axé, the other path to atonement is sacrifice, for atonement is detachment from all longings and self-centered attitudes.*

> *Once one is liberated from mortal desires, and sublimates passion into motivation, one can connect with the spirit's eternal True Will. Which is for us to actualize our Superheru form and our Superself, when are minds and bodies shall be perfected, and our Sanctification Mission is fulfilled."*

As I meditated later that night on the smiling face of Krstjah, I in I saw and felt his aura flow into me, and fill me with a bubbling euphoria. I awoke the next day and found that my skin now sparkled gold, and I in I give thanks still for Krstjah filling my EMF and soul amphora!

My shine became more and more obvious in the ever more gray and dreary region we were visiting, where the sky was blackening from greed. A fog of exhaust fumes was as high as the tallest skyscraper, and nature was so uprooted and replaced that I hardly saw a tree. Lord Binah's companies were in the middle of this destruction of the land, and the taxes he paid to Iset made his company's vital to the empire. Yet Lord Binah knew that it was he who was indebted to Iset's goodwill, even for his life, and thus Binah had backstabbed me in order to avoid the fire.

Iset hired the infamous *Scorpius X-1*, a devilish man who had become part cyborg in order to befit his assassin lifestyle. Krstjah and I would meet him and Binah on the 13th level of Binah's skyscraper, which was guarded by the statue of a multi-headed crocodile. We had arrived on the day of the Council on Financial Relations, when the 13 richest people in Kismet met to talk shop. Inside the building was a bare and granite lobby, an elevator, and a tall, bident shaped fountain, with a crystal orb floating on top.

After our long elevator ascent, we beheld Lord Binah's lavish penthouse, with floor to ceiling windows, and rhodochrosite floor tiles. The prosperous members gathered sat round a golden table next to their aides, who were all clones of beautiful celebrities and always smiled. Among the members was Scorpius X-1 in disguise, and he sat in front of an aquarium with seahorses and sea butterflies. Scorpius was not the only one there with inhuman parts, for the men gathered had spent millions in order to artificially prolong their lives.

Binah warmly welcomed Krstjah and I, and after we were seated, he asked where I had been for nearly twenty years. I told him that I was on a quest that was nearly over, and as I told him about my lord and friend Krstjah, I cried joyous tears. Binah was unmoved by my passion, and mentioned that Emperor Iset was said to be on the hunt for one with blackened skin.

I then said, "The righteous have no concern for the schemes of Caesars or tyrants, for we are marching onto our glory, and they onto their end." Binah then asked if I had plans to return to my kingdom of

Bharata, and live once again as a wealthy and beloved saint king. I then said, "I in I have sacrificed all worldy attachments and desires, so that in the emptiness of my heart I in I can hear my soul sing."

Lord Binah said, "I have always rejected that notion of charity, because it goes against your own idea of karma and reward. I was blessed with a rich family because of my past life, you say, and I say I then used strategy to maximize that award."

I reminded Binah that though his past life karma had in fact rewarded him much, to whom much is given, much is expected. Binah said, "Again you spew this spiritual mumbo-jumbo in front of this group of hard-working winners, and again I reject it. It is every man's right to obtain what he desires, and to enjoy what he obtains, because, unlike you, I believe you only live once. And, if I were to concern myself with an unconfirmed afterlife and give up all the wealth and power I deserve, I would be a dunce."

I said, "Beloved, I in I speak from the sincerest love, when I in I warn thee that self-centeredness is the putrefaction of the soul. It is this self-centeredness, even more than the lusts themselves, which one must detach from if one is to become a sun that is astral.

"Beloved, we can purify our desires and longings if we but make them spiritual, and make them the greatest motivation and passion. If we be desirous of only the good and righteous way, our base energies then become kundalini, and not our soul's own assassin. Beloved, the rewards for this compassionate way lie not only in the afterlife, but here and now, for detachment leads to true bliss. When the empty and endless lust for power and possessions is replaced with the joy of heroic altruism, and the heart rises from the Deep abyss."

As I saw Crovin land inconspicuously on an opal gargoyle statue outside the window, Scorpius X-1 was triggered into action. He rose suddenly to his feet, and from a gun built into his forearm, he fired a specially built bullet that was made of nanite fractions. I know not what came over me, but I distinctly recall my body beginning to move towards Krstjah as soon as Scorpius had started. I moved in front of Krstjah just in time, and the bullet entered my heart, and separated just as my body and soul parted.

Each tiny machine carried the last of the venom of Apothis which Iset had received from the Ark of Tessarasa, and they filled my body with the toxin. Yet, by grace and the Intelligence of the Heart, my soul had unlocked the *Idi of Astral Projection*, as it is described in our *doctrine*.

A brilliant burst of rainbow light shot out from my flesh, and blinded the Council on Financial Relations for 13 whole seconds. When again they could see, they beheld me as a blackened rainbow light body inside a circular rainbow aura, and thus began my legend.

Scorpius' robotic eyes had managed to adjust during my Baptism of Light, and I saw him through the light as he fled and escaped. Krstjah immediately understood that my soul was now free to roam, and said that he was proud that my Superheru form had awaked.

With tears in his eyes, and a smile yet still on his beautiful face, Krstjah thanked me for saving his life, and told me he loved me. His sincere words were enough to transform my disorientation into a transcendent joy, and I said, "Lord Krstjah, my love itself is thee."

The council members there were transfigured by my lustration and light, and they bowed down and made obeisances before me. As their skin and tears reflected my rainbow coat of many colors, they vowed to sacrifice all their wealth to Krstjah and charity.

Krstjah was pleased by their Sanctification Mission, and vowed to punish my assassin as soon as he first defeated Iset, his nemesis. I recalled I had disclosed the hiding place of Queen Tuya before the ears of Scorpius, and I asked Krstjah to first go protect his family from that menace. Krstjah agreed, and decided to return to and reconquer his homeland of Nubitopia, and protect his family, before defeating Iset. Lord Binah would turn his land into a city called Rastari Town, or Reston, and it became a famous model of a green, ecological city for big cities across Kismet.

Before Krstjah and I parted ways, I promised to watch over and protect him from the astral dimension, and he asked me a favor. He asked that I return to my love, Selene, and the Moonstone Palace, and fulfill the promise to return to her that I had gave her.

I smiled as he asked me two more favors: to have faith in his victory, and to enjoy the Nirvana which I had received with Herudom. I promised to obey him, yet I promised him that after I had done as he instructed, I would heroically use my new idis and astral freedom.

After I returned to Selene and explained my form, she understood, and we were wed together in a moonlight ceremony. Now, I in I am called the Holy Ghost, and I bring compassion to anyone in need during a full moon; and with Selene's help, I in I wrote this testimony.

Heru Krstjah, Heru Krstjah,
Krstjah Krstjah, Heru Heru.
Heru Rastar, Heru Rastar,
Rastar Rastar, Heru Heru.
Axé!

Glossary

A *aru: noun*
The simulation of heaven which is tailored to each individual.

A *ghora: 15, noun*
The spiritual underworld which dead souls wander through until their lives and spirits are judged.

A *gartha: 15, noun*
The physical underworld that consists of precious mineral and pristine water, which can be entered only by a righteous elect who can live much longer than average lives under the light of their sun, Rahu. The seven entrances to Agartha, are typically located in hidden underground caverns, and are guarded by either mythical beasts or monsters of different varieties.

A *lchemy: 67, noun*
The science of natural mysticism and metaphysics concerned with perfecting the human soul through spiritual, chemical, psychological, tantric, and especially symbolic means. The aim is to emulate the principals and laws which govern nature and express themselves on every level of existence, especially in the microcosm which is the body, mind, and spirit of man. The goal of alchemy is to make one's soul or self as permanent or everlasting as gold through one's good deeds and transcendent experiences and wisdom and thus legacy. Through the wedding of both a science of symbols and the law of correspondences, in addition to a belief that faith itself is a magical elixir, alchemists create a personal mythology whose interpretation guides their daily activities and communal festivities.

A *lmighty: 12, noun*
    A name for The I, the Most High, the One unity which includes and envelops all things in creation. Symbolized as a glass sphere in Delight, the 13th dimension.

A *nkh Wedja Senub: 46, noun*
    "Live Long, Healthy, and Prosper."

A *tonement: 179, noun*
    To have the I Am awareness, an egoless identification with the environment.

A *vatar: 18, noun*
    A physical body which is occupied by a Principal; also, a living being which is a manifestation, creation, or duplication of a Principal; also, a living being which is the primarily a representation or symbol of the Almighty.

A *xe´: 11, exclamation, invocation, adverb*
    Said at the beginning of statements as a call and response to mean "Give thanks and praise!;" also, to mean "Give onto me the power to perform, if it be your will, Almighty;" also, said at end of prayers as a thanksgiving that it is done; also, said after invocations to certain Principals in order to spiritually affirm and conclude invitation

Bad Faith: 121, noun
Any activity that goes against the precepts of one's Faith, religion, self-discipline, or consciously desired choices and goals. To do what one knows one should not do, as if one is forced to do this incorrect action by the force of habit or addiction or weak discipline or parasites, is Bad Faith. To not do what one knows one should do is also Bad Faith.

Baptism of the Heart: 80, noun
The process in which one's EMF is expanded after an expansion of their love and compassion, and a contraction of their self-centeredness and egotism. This is the first major step towards enlightenment in the Path to Herudom. An example would be after a person becomes a parent.

Baptism of Fire: 155, noun
The first major, climactic test for the soul on the path of enlightenment and herudom. This coincides with the 'Atonement with Father' step in the hero's journey. Every preceding step has been a guidepost, but this step is a full on test and trial and ordeal. The soul must prove its sincerity in its quest for perfection, and it must do so with determination and the degree of wisdom and discipline it has already achieved so far on the path.

This ordeal is typically related to inherited struggles, such as racial injustice or sexism or economic exploitation or revenge. Even more specifically, these struggles are typically psychological in nature, such as drug abuse or self-confidence or feelings of self-worth or isolation or abandonment or resilience. This Baptism is a purifying crucible, and it is the first form of the perfection and purification which is to come later on the path. It is also the first 'Sanctification Mission,' in that it inevitably involves overcoming or incorporating some aspect of the self's shadow and negative aspects.

After overcoming this ordeal, the individual feels invigorated to continue on the path to altruism and perfection. They are filled with self-confidence and determination, and new knowledge of the depth of their powers to overcome. They will have finally sacrificed or overcome certain limitations which had held them back; again, this is a preview of the more dramatic Perfection and Purification to come.

Bedroom of the Bride: *116, noun*
The stage in one's enlightenment that occurs during the activation of the third eye chakra, before the awakening of the Idi of the Eye, in which one must face one's nemesis.

Benay ha elohim: *41, noun*
Sons of the Almighty.

Bindi: *77, noun*
A colored dot placed between the eyebrows or in the middle of the forehead, to represent the Third Eye.

Biophotonic aura: *161, noun*
The aura that surrounds a person, created by the barely visible photons or light particles which the body produces as a form of bioluminescence.

Celestial Sea: 15, noun
     The sky, which contains the physical bodies of the Celestials, and is encapsulated inside of a dome which separates the Celestial Sea from Shambhala, the spiritual home of the Celestial Principals.

Celestials: 15, noun
     The name for the Principals which are anthrompomorphizations of the planets of the solar system, including the Sun, Moon, Saturn, etc.

Consort: 32, noun
     The non-human, animal and beast spirits which accompany the Principals and some angelic Iyrins.

Deep: 15, noun
     The lowest level of Zion, and a dark and deep, boiling ocean that cleanses the karma of damned spirits. In the center of the Deep grows a red, white, and golden lotus flower, and all of the higher planes of Zion rest on top of the flower.

Delight: 12, noun
     The unimaginable and unknowable and theoretical 13th or last dimension outside of all forms of time and space which is the true home or center of the Almighty. Symbolized as an infinite space of white light.

Demijinn: 22, noun
Kathol Iset; or any person that is half-human and half-devil.

Demonatry: noun
Commonly referred to as energy vampirism or energy zombie. The practice of receiving spiritual energy, and thus healing and vitality, at the expense of others. When a person receives energy directly or indirectly by directly or indirectly causing the decrease of positive energy in another person, typically someone that they encounter on a regular basis. This energy may or may not come directly from the victim, but the increase of energy in one is correlated to the decrease in the victim. Sacrifices are forms of demonatry, for instance.

While it only gives the attacker a momentary boast of energy, it also slowly increases their energy generally over time, while decreasing the victim's general soul frequency proportionate to the energy that is stolen times the energy it loses during the karmic reactions to this lowering of soul frequency or positivity.

Divine Assumption: 152, noun
When one wholly identifies with the I, such that their ego is completely silenced, and their soul feels at one with the universe.

EMF (ecomorphic field): 73, noun
One of the seven components of the soul, the ecomorphic field is a 'subtle' or metaphysical or soul-powered energy that surrounds the soul and heart and body. The size of the field depends on one's

spiritual development and enlightenment. Whatever is inside of this field becomes psychically knowable to the heart's neurons- the Intelligence of the Heart. This field is responsible for the Idis of the Heart, such as Intuition, Charm, and Stamina.

E *psilon state: 171, noun*
The epsilon state of consciousness is a very low-frequency brainwave. This is the state yogis go into when they achieve "suspended animation." In this state, western medical doctors will no longer perceive a heartbeat, respiration or pulse. The left and right brain hemispheres become synchronized, and one has the feelings of wholeness and atonement.

E *ther: 14, noun*
A slightly denser or more physical form of the most basic spiritual energy. Symbolized as being a transparent and smoky plasma.

F *low of the Heart: 106, noun*
An expressive performance or activity that is done in the 'flow-state,' in which one becomes completely immersed in what one is focusing on and doing, such that the usual chatter of the mind is removed and the full possibilities of one's creativity and intuition are unleashed.

G *ratitude Tuning Ritual: 138*
The main 'manifestation' ritual of the Rastari, it is a ritual or spiritual practice in which one connects with the feeling of being

grateful for having an object or state desired, as if one has already obtained the object in question. If one desires a 2024 Mercedes G-Wagon, one not only imagines and visualizes already having the G-Wagon, but also feels the feeling of being grateful that one already has the G-Wagon.

Hemogoblin: 149, noun
    A mutated branch of humanity, whose body does not produce iron, and who

Herudom: 183, noun
    Enlightenment; immortality of the soul; completion of one's Sanctification Mission; the Idi of Solvation; to be Solved.

Holy Spirit: 12, noun
    The most pervasive dimension of creation, and the energy source of the physical and spiritual universes, which is like a living network or ocean or web of metaphysical energy. This network is the creation of Shekinga Shira, the imagination and power of the Almighty in our universe. All things are only illusory and temporal and shifting forms of the Holy Spirit. It is most similar to a divine and omnipotent version of the unconscious of the psyche, and the intuition and psychic abilities of the soul, and the energy of the spirit, and the unlimited power of the imagination.

The I: 12, noun

A name for the Almighty, the Most High, One unity which includes and envelops all things in creation. Symbolized as a transparent glass sphere in Delight, the 13th dimension; also, a name for the members of the Rastari community, and members of any Faith which is henotheistic.

I *di: 22, noun*
A psychic ability which may affect one's self, others, or one's environment. 13 idis in total, and their effects defer in different people.
Idi of Akashic Access: 176, noun
The psychic ability to astrally witness, or intuitively know, or receive a 'download of information' on any past events and any already understood knowledge;

I *di of Astral Projection*: 180, noun
The psychic ability to move through space-time in the astral dimension beyond the normal limits of the mikarbod. This includes remote viewing, appearing as an apparition, appearing in another's dream, advanced lucid dreaming, communicating with the spirits that reside in the astral dimension, and reconnecting to one's physical body after extended periods apart.

I *dis of the Eye:* 134, noun
These are the final six psychic abilities which are fueled by the Third Eye and pineal gland. Including Astral Projection, Akashic Access, Improbability, Solvation, Nirvana, and Transfusion.

I *di of Charm: 86, noun*
The psychic ability to totally influence and partially hypnotize others. Relates to one's ability to resonant with EMF of another, such that one's ideas and directions become more agreeable to the other person's mind and will.

I *dis of the Heart: 80, noun*
These are the seven psychic abilities which are fueled by the EMF. Including, Charm (the ability to influence and hypnotize others), Healing, Intuition, Stamina, Supersense, Telekinesis, Telepathy, and Transfiguration (the ability to slightly alter one's body features, including height, weight, buoyancy, physical age, and facial features).

I *di of Improbability*: 176, noun
The psychic ability which allows one to seem as though they have miraculously good luck and fortune, and which gives one the unconscious ability to 'Manifest' at extraordinary or miraculous levels.

I *di of Nirvana*: 179, noun
The psychic ability in which one has complete control over one's emotional state. Also, the ability to heal and create the feeling of ecstasy or serenity in another.

I *di of Solvation: 136, noun*
To be solved, to be saved. The ultimate idi, and the Toll for Immortality, received after one's completed their ordained 'soul

service,' the duties of their soul to the will of the Almighty. This gives a soul access to one of the seven heavens which do not confer eternal and everlasting immortality, such as the heaven of the Sun. A soul may be permitted to exist in these heavens for hundreds of thousands of years in Kismet time, but the soul will be reborn, unless it achieves access to the eighth heaven- the afterlife on Sirius- where everlasting souls reside until the end of this form of the physical and spiritual universe.

I *di of Stamina: 85, noun*
The psychic ability that allows to be have superhuman endurance, durability, fasting ability, and allows one to live far beyond the average age. The ability relates to one's breathing, and from one's ability to power one's EMF and physical body with the orgone energy in the environment.

I *di of Supersense: 155, noun*
The psychic ability that gives one superhuman athletic abilities and physical prowess, especially for limited amounts of time.

I *di of Telepathy: 111, noun*
The psychic ability to sense and comprehend the thoughts in another's mind, and also to input thoughts and commands into another's mind.

I *di of Transfiguration:*
Transfiguration is the natural psychic ability of shapeshifters, but it also includes any instance in which the body's physical

characteristics change in metaphysical and dramatic ways. This includes a dramatic change in weight, facial features, hair color, and even height in extreme cases. Strangest of all is the random ability to lower or increase one's density, such that one becomes lighter when running and heavier whilst at rest.

I di of Transfusion (to transfuse): 155, noun
The psychic ability to momentarily become an avatar or conduit for a Principal, and thereby utilize some of that Principal's supernatural powers for psychic effects. Also, the ability to transmute physical atoms and molecules, and reshape form to create new forms, such as pure gold; also the ability to imprint spiritual energy into physical objects. Also, the ability to permanently leave the body, or physical death, when one consciously decides to.

This is the psychic ability through which the most dramatic physical abilities are exercised. By tapping into the brain state of the principal or natural element, the individual is granted supernatural abilities. Pyrokinesis, flying, transmutation, high level transfiguration and shape-shifting, walking on water, advanced regeneration and healing, super strength or durability, advanced akashic access, weather control, speaking with spirits or astral entities, etc, all come from Transfusion.

I ntelligence of the Heart: 164, noun
This the result of the full activation of the Third Eye and the crown chakra, when the intelligence of the brain connects with the wisdom contained within the neurons of the heart. The heart's nervous system, also known as the "intrinsic cardiac nervous system" or "heart brain", contains around 40,000 neurons called sensory neurites. These neurons are similar to those found in the brain. The heart's nervous

system can process information independently of the brain and nervous system, but when the heart and brain work together, you get the Intelligence of the Heart.

I *nicestor: 14, noun*
The name for the five Principals which represent everlasting guiding laws of existence, including: the principle of time- Ihah Eternity, the principle of space- Ihum Infinity, the principle of rhythm- Irie Ragas, the principle of correspondence- Ites Ragas, the principle of our universe- Ion.

I *T: 13, noun*
A name for Jewhuti Maat Mawenzi, the omniscience of the Almighty.

I *yrin: noun*
Iyrin - ancient Ethiopian word for angel. The Iyrin is the guardian angel and higher self of the soul. The Iyrin is the result of the cluster of ideals which the Superself of the soul most yearns to emulate, be it a cluster of courage or valor or wisdom or compassion. The Iyrin is typically depicted as an idealized and sanctified version of the self, including either glowing auras or wings or mudras. The Iyrin is also the intermediary between the soul and the Neter which the soul most embodies.

I *yrin Form: 139, noun*

Similar to the physical Superheru Form, the Iyrin Form is the version of the mikarbod or astral body in which the body is enriched with the blackness of the Holy Spirit, and resembles the body of Krstjah. The skin becomes as black as night, and the hair becomes as golden as sunlight. The individual often has 2 or 4 wings as well.

J *apamala: 105, noun*
A loop of prayer beads commonly used in spiritual practices.

K *RST: 29, noun*
A christ like individual. A crown chakra activated, or pineal gland activated, or Enlightened one, who has activated their Superheru form. Such a person always has the Almighty on their mind, and can thus alchemically purify any karma from their actions. Such a person seems obsessed or overwhelmingly dedicated to the revelation of the god-power or psychic abilities within them, and they are continuously seeking perfection of body and soul. Such a person is driven by their True Will towards their Solved Destiny and Toll for Immortality, and is thus heroic in some manner.

K *achina: 158, noun*
The ancestral spirit beings of certain Faiths which are said to interact with and possess humans, especially during dances and festivals.

K *emet: 76, noun*
The ancient name of Egypt.

Kumkum: *77, noun*
   A powder made of turmeric or other materials, that is used for social and especially religious markings.

Kismet: *15, noun*
   The plane and planet of existence on which we live; also, a name for Earth.

Lambda state: *171, noun*
   Lambda waves are very high frequency brainwaves, associated with wholeness and atonement, as well as with mystical and out of body experiences. Lambda states of consciousness are associated with the ability of certain sects of Tibetan monks who can mediate in the Himalayan mountains in sub-zero temperatures wearing little clothing and maintaining a hot body temperature which melts the snow around them.

Law of Correspondence: *59, noun*
   Ites Rajas, the Principal of Correspondence; also, "as above, so below" and "as within, so without."

Lunar month: *27, noun*
   In the Rastari lunar calendar, there are 13 months of twenty-eight days. There is an annual 'day outside of time' on July 25th of the Gregorian calendar, and the first day of the first moon month is

July 26th. The fourth lunar month is from October 18th - November 14th

M*aat: 53, noun*
    A philosophical concept that embodies truth, justice, balance, harmony, order, law, and moral reciprocity.

M*agician: noun*
    one who has awakened one of the Idis of the Eye; one who works with the Generative principle, or Shekinga and the Holy spirit- or the quantum field of possibilities- in order to generate favorable preconceived outcomes or physical actualities.

M*etatron's Cube: 161, noun*
    One of the most important symbols in sacred geometry, it is a three dimensional geometric symbol that contains 13 circles connected by straight lines, which together form all of the five Platonic solids.

M*ikarbod: 41, noun*
    One of the seven components of a soul, which is known as a light body or astral body, and allows one to traverse the astral realms of dreams, imagination, and transcendent visions.

M*t. Meru: 15, noun*

The mountain in the center of Kismet, on the island of Atlantis, which is only visible and accessible to a righteous elect. At its base is the Tree of Life, and one of the gates to Agartha.

Mysticism: noun
the realization that the responsibility and leadership of ones soul and salvation is inside oneself. That the divine is not outside, but inside of the soul. And following this, the many means in which mankind brings the divine from the external into the internal, from the otherworldly into the inner-worldly. Principles of these systems are alchemy and mystical religions, and all forms of creative disciplined livity with the goal of becoming a mirror and copy of the god living within oneself.

Neter: 11, noun
A name for the Almighty, who is the ultimate Neter for all souls. Also, one's individual Neter is the Principal which the Superself- the eternal, virtually existing soul- derives from. Every soul is only but a duplication and derivation of the first souls of existence- which are the Omnicestors, the Inicestors, and the Celestial Principals- and the specific Principal from which one's Superself ultimately derives from is one's Neter.

None: 14, noun
All of the spiritual energy which fills the Holy Spirit, the 12th dimension. Symbolized as an infinite ocean of vibrating energy, which sits beneath a sky of smoke like ether.

Omnicestor: 12, noun
The name for the three Principals which represent the omniscience, omnipresence, and omnipotence of the Almighty: Shekinga Shira, Akasha Kibo, and Jewhuti Maat Mawenzi.

Orgone energy: 69, noun
Prana, chi, reiki, Planck energy, etc. This is the physical energy which correlates to the metaphysical or spiritual energy of the Holy Spirit. It is especially prevalent in high elevations, and in natural spaces that are near large bodies of water.

Padmasana: 68, noun
The lotus yoga posture, in which the crossed feet rest on the opposing shin or thigh.

Peter: noun
In Rasayana, pets are not simply personal property of the family, but are instead representatives or agents or avatars of certain Principals and principles of nature. To make this distinction clear, they are called 'Peters' and not pets. Dogs, for instance, are avatars of the Principal Shai Royg Bivi, the god of the family, of the home, of loyalty, of one's guardian angel, of the Taurus constellation, and of simple pleasures. Cats are avatars of either Adomah Sekkemi aka Aries, or of Kairos Ra Stari aka the Sun and Leo. As such, pets are to be highly respected and cared for, as if one is caring for a living god.

Pranayama: 85, noun
   An ancient breath technique and yogic practice that involves controlling your breath in different styles and lengths.

Principal: 12, noun
   A personification and anthropomorphization of certain aspects of universal and natural principles, which combines concepts with physical and spiritual items such as planets, zodiac signs, tarot cards, etc. These Principals are merely symbols of aspects of the one true entity, the Most High, Almighty, I.

Rahu: 17, noun
   The sunned moon of Agartha, with a moon-like light which provides heat like a sun, and is responsible for solar and lunar eclipses through its shadow twin, Ketu.

Rasayana: 88, noun
   A Sanskrit word that means "path of essence", and was used as a term for alchemy; also, the mystical dance of Krstjah; also, the official term for the Rastari faith, for whom it means: the spiritual practice of seeking heroic redemption with the goal of achieving spiritual immortality, achieved by the faith in the spiritual truth of the symbolic reality explained in the Rastari Saga, and by living according to the laws of the spiritual system.

Samadhi: 40, noun

A deep state of meditative consciousness and contemplation, that is free from ego-generated thoughts and emotions, and is characterized by joy, calm, and mental alertness. The brain often reaches the epsilon or lambda brain frequency. In this state, one may easily and regularly experience psychic phenomena such as precognition, lucid dreaming, and astral projection.

Sanctification Mission: *179, noun*
The duty, service, or set of actions which one was ordained to perform in order to achieve Herudom and Solvation, which is the immortality of the soul. This mission is typically one that the individual consciously decides to perform at some point in the Path to Herudom or Path to Enlightenment, whether or not they create the mission or are given the mission from a spiritual leader.

Selah: *11, exclamation, invocation, adverb*
Said at the end of statements or prayers or obeisances to mean "Give thanks that it is done, if it be the will of the Almighty;" also, said during conversations to indicate that one has received insight and overstanding

Shaman: *161, noun*
A person regarded as having access to, and influence in, the astral dimension aka the world of spirits, who typically uses trance, song, mantras, and herbal medicines during rituals, and practices divination and healing and communicating with animals.

S *hambhala: 15, noun*
The spiritual home of the Celestial Principals, and the highest plane of existence in Zion.

S *hema Omega: 112, noun*
The Rastari version of 'aum,' and one of the most common mantras of Rasayana. Involves deep breathing and deep exhalations, whilst repeating the mantra ' Haum Raum.' Also used during Dragon's Breath ritual.

S *hri yantra: 91, noun*
A form of mystical diagram that comprises nine interlocking triangles that form 43 smaller triangles in concentric levels. The form symbolizes many aspects of divinity and the cosmos, and its projection into three dimensions results in the image of Mt. Meru.

S *olved: 165,* noun
To have achieved the Idi of Solvation, Herudom, and immortality of the soul.

S *oma: 84, noun*
A drink made from monoatomic gold.

S *oul: noun*

Completed upon birth, and dismantled after death and judgement, the soul is centered around the human heart, and made up of the following seven parts:

1 . I in I:
The I in In is the individual ion - or light code of spirit information- of the Almighty which is identical to itself and exists in all things. Essentially, the I in I is a brand or trademark of the Almighty, and it exists within all things.

2 . Kama:
The kama of the soul is the spiritual energy which energizes the soul. It is similar to the term 'ka' or the life-force or the animating breath, and it corresponds to and feeds off of the external energy which has been called prana and chi. The kama of the soul can grow or diminish in its power based on the practices and thoughts of the soul, and this energy is stored in the EMF of the soul. The death of the body only occurs after there is no more kama in the soul.

3 . EMF:
The ecomorphic field is the torus field of spirit which is the outer layer of the soul. It has been called 'aura,' and it is essentially our 'true individual spirit.' It is the cloud of spirit that individuates one spirit entity from another.

The EMF is in between energy and information, for it both stores the soul's spiritual energy, and it stores the memories and information of the soul's previous incarnations. While the EMF changes through the different soul incarnations through the actions of the embodied soul, the EMF is the most everlasting aspect of our souls that is individual to our spirit.

If the soul does not reach immortality and Solvation, only its EMF container shall remain after its time in the afterlife or the Deep. It is through the traces of past lives in the EMF that it can be said that our true spirit, the Superself, is on a journey of evolution from soul incarnation to soul incarnation.

The energy of the EMF is also responsible for half of all psychic abilities, which we call the Idis of Heart.

4. The Mind Trinity:

Just as there are 3 places in the body which store and use neurons, there are actually 3 different minds in humans, and this mind trinity is the most informational, and thus most mundane, part of the soul. The strongest and most influential part of this trinity has been called the unconscious, the instinctual mind, or the gut brain. It stores ones longterm memories, cultural programming, and biological responses. The next part of the trinity has been called the emotions, and we call it the Intelligence of the Heart, or the heart mind, as it controls ones heart rate and breathing, as well as ones emotional responses. The last part of the mind trinity is typically confused to be the entire mind, and has been called the brain. It controls and stores short-term memories, the executive functioning of the body, and is the generator of the ego.

5. Shaya:

The shaya of the soul is the information which controls the physical image of the individual. It can be thought of as one's spiritual shadow, and as the spiritual correspondence of the body; this means that the body itself is in fact a temporary but essential part of the soul, and not simply a vehicle for the soul. The information of the shaya determines the individual's physical size and characteristics. The shaya of living beings naturally adjusts over time as the individual ages and grows, however it can also adjust rapidly, as can be seen in nature in shapeshifters such as octopuses and thanks to psychic abilities.

6. Mikarbod:
Also known as the merkabah, the astral body, or the higher self. This is a duplication of the soul, like the soul in a parallel dimension. The mikarbod allows the soul to exist and operate in the astral dimensions of dreams, deep imagination and visualization, deep meditation, remote viewing, astral projection. It is through the mikarbod that the soul may receive and transmit spiritual communication and information, such as mediumship, telepathy, and akashic access. The mikarbod contains the intelligence of the Superself, or the traces of the past soul incarnations of the individual spirit.

7. I of I:
Also known as the 'I' and the Self, the I of I is the conscious identity and will of the soul. The I of I is the 'I' one is referring to when one thinks of one's self or one's own consciousness; it is the observer of every thought and the aspect which seems to make conscious decisions in the eternal now. The I of I is the sum total of all of the other parts of the soul, and as the other parts of the soul change, so does the I of I slightly change in correspondence. The ultimate goal of Rasayana, then, is the perfection of this part of the soul, for we believe that eternal life of the soul has been promised to those who enlighten and perfect their sense of self or I of I. This perfection takes knowledge, awareness, intention, discipline, and the fulfillment of the duty of the soul, which results in the heroic or Superheru version of the I of I.

S ouljahs: 43, Noun
A spiritually or morally righteous warrior; also, a warrior loyal to Krstjah Rastari.

S un Namaskar: 132, noun
Surya Namaskar, or Sun Salutation. A yoga practice that involves a sequence of 12 linked poses, or asanas, as a way to honor the sun and to help sync a person's physical cycles with the sun's, which can take around 12.25 years to complete.

S uperheru Form: 182, noun
Similar to the astral or spiritual Iyrin Form, the Superheru Form is the version of the physical body in which the body is enriched with the power and blackness of the Holy Spirit, and looks like Krstjah's body. The skin becomes as black as night, and the hair becomes as golden as sunlight. This transformation is often accompanied by other variations in one's form, varying from person to person. Even animals can achieve their Superheru Form under certain conditions.

S uperself: 23, noun
The final and highest version of a soul-spirit, which already exists, but only virtually, until it is actualized when one of the spirit's many soul incarnations achieves Herudom and the Idi of Solvation which is the Toll for Immortality. Then the soul-spirit will actualize its Superself, and will be able to remember all of its previous soul

incarnations.

In addition, the Superself is also the intelligence of the spirit without a personality (soul, ego, self-awareness), the cause of the form of the Iyrin and Neter, the traces of the past lives or soul incarnations, what is referred to as the higher self, the messenger of spiritual information, the usual 'other' in non-lucid dreams, the intelligence of the unconscious mind.

*S*ynchronicity: 116, noun
The natural yet miraculous condition in which two or more mental or physical phenomena with no discoverable causal connection appear to coincide in time, and this conincidence appears to have a metaphysical or spiritual meaning. Synchronicity provides experiential proof of the spiritual or psychic or astral dimension, as much as quantum entanglement provides empirical proof of the scientific 'ether,' which is a web of elemental energy in which information can travel instantaneously.

*T*ree of Life: 15, noun
An ancient and everlasting tree as big as a mountain which sits in a cavern as big as the Grand Canyon. At its base is the main entrance to Agartha.

*T*rue Believer: 54, noun
A person with the utmost faith and conviction in a particular set of spiritual concepts and beliefs.

T*rue Will: 41, noun*
The one true aspiration of every Superself and embodied spirit; to actualize its immortality and escape the endless simulation of souls.

U*mans (Umanaintapys)*: noun, 167
Degenerated humans who have lived underground for centuries, and have access to advanced technology such as UFO's and cyborgs and cloning. Most so-called aliens from outer space are actually a form or type of Uman, including the Grays and the Reptillians and the Pleadians.

U*ncertainty*: 154, noun
The uncertainty principle, also known as Heisenberg's indeterminacy principle, is a fundamental concept in quantum mechanics. It states that there is a limit to the precision with which certain pairs of physical properties, such as position and momentum, can be simultaneously known. Ultimately, it predicts that particles can appear or form out of seeming empty space, under certain circumstances.

Z*ion: 15, noun*
Our physically and spiritually accessible universe, symbolized as a sphere which contains seven planes of existence.

Don't miss out!

Visit the website below and you can sign up to receive emails whenever Ras Heru King publishes a new book. There's no charge and no obligation.

https://books2read.com/r/B-A-IEAX-NEVFC

BOOKS 2 READ

Connecting independent readers to independent writers.

Katalize.Net

About the Publisher

We are a creative studio specializing in visionary fiction and afro-indigenous-futurism, and our goal is to be the leader of a new genre of entertainment called popular spiritual fiction and popular mythical fiction. Ultimately, our goal is to create new appreciation for spirituality and to create spaces for the growth of spiritual communities. Our motto is,

Transforming Visions and Dreams into Realities and Teams!
Read more at www.katalize.net.